The Death
of
Marlon Brando

The Death
of
Marlon Brando

PIERRE GOBEIL

Translated and with a Foreword by

Steven Urquhart

Library and Archives Canada Cataloguing in Publication

Gobeil, Pierre

[Mort de Marlon Brando. English]

    The death of Marlon Brando : a novel / Pierre Gobeil ; Steven Urquhart.

Translation of: La mort de Marlon Brando.
ISBN 978-1-55096-313-7

    I. Urquhart, Steven, 1974- II. Title. III Title: Mort de Marlon Brando. English.

PS8563.O24M6713 2013   C843'.6   C2013-900140-9

Design and Composition by Mishi Oroboros
Typeset in American Typewriter and Birka at the Moons of Jupiter Studios

Published by Exile Editions Ltd ~ www.ExileEditions.com
144483 Southgate Road 14 – GD, Holstein, Ontario, N0G 2A0
Printed and Bound in Canada by Imprimerie Gauvin

We acknowledge the financial support of the Government of Canada through the
National Translation Program for Book Publishing for our translation activities. We
would also like to acknowledge the Canada Council for the Arts, the Government of
Canada through the Canada Book Fund (CBF), the Ontario Arts Council, and the
Ontario Media Development Corporation, for our overall publishing activities.

Canadian Sales: The Canadian Manda Group, 165 Dufferin Street,
Toronto ON M6K 3H6   www.mandagroup.com   416 516 0911

North American and International Distribution, and U.S. Sales:
Independent Publishers Group, 814 North Franklin Street,
Chicago IL 60610   www.ipgbook.com   toll free: 1 800 888 4741

CONTENTS

FOREWORD
by Steven Urquhart

Originally published in French in 1989, *La mort de Marlon Brando* has received relatively little critical attention despite being listed as one of a hundred must-read Quebecois novels by Nota bene Editions. Whether it be the novel's troubling content or its enigmatic title, the reasons for this lack of attention are unclear and simply regrettable. Indeed, one cannot help but see the injustice of this situation when, according to well-known Quebecois journalist and literary critic Gilles Marcotte, the story has "no weaknesses and doesn't back down before the unfolding drama of an abandoned child. It reminds you of Steinbeck, Yves Thériault."

Such praise demonstrates the merits of Pierre Gobeil's novel, in which a young narrator called Charles relives the events leading up to his assault by a mentally handicapped farmhand, named *Him*. *The Death of Marlon Brando* deals tactfully with this delicate topic by focusing on the difficulty of expressing the unspeakable and insisting on the power of suggestion. As such, the question of "translation" in the sense of interpretation is at the centre of the novel, in which Charles struggles to communicate his angst and inner turmoil in relation to the farmhand as they coexist and carry out their respective duties on his parents' land. Unable to speak to his parents, who ignore him and who trust their employee, Charles is disempowered and thus remains silent for the most part in the story. As the narrator of the novel, however, he does seem to find a voice which he uses to finally understand and explain what happened to him over the course of a summer. Although this may not be clear at the beginning of the work, the attentive reader realizes little by little that Charles is not simply describing his traumatic experience, but that he is also reliving it. We see this when he combines his thoughts at the time of the actual events with retrospective considerations dealing with what he did not say, or write in a school composition assigned for the summer break. In this way, the novel speaks more by what is *not* said than by what actually is.

A composite work, Charles' summer homework assignment acts like a cinema voice-off in the novel. Structured like Francis Ford Coppola's celebrated film, *Apocalypse Now*, based on Joseph Conrad's novel *Heart of Darkness*, the composition not only explains the title of Gobeil's book, but conveys the sinister nature of events in the novel. In other words, the film, in which Marlon Brando's character Colonel Kurtz is assassinated by a U.S. sergeant in the closing scene, reflects the fact that Charles is being stalked by a maleficent worker. This situation, which is misunderstood by his teachers who fail to recognize the film's metaphoric quality within the text, invites readers to infer meaning in the text and pay attention to the nature of any given utterance or lack thereof. While serving as a guide to the reader who must contend with the novel's disjointed sequence of events, the film and thus the composition also highlight Charles' feelings of abandonment, betrayal and helplessness.

Indeed, despite being more oblique than the narrative discourse, the vacation assignment allows Charles to name names, so to speak, and explain that which he cannot or does not want to admit, such as the farmhand's monstrous character. Calling him an *ornithorynchus*, Latin for "platypus," in the composition, Charles' indirectly describes the anonymous French-Canadian antagonist's strange behaviour and speech mannerisms. Unnameable in ways, Him effectively embodies this unusual and hybrid "beast." Acting at once like an animal and then a child, despite being an adult, he also speaks in a roundabout fashion, using incorrect, foreign or invented words, which trouble the narrator. Disconcerted by Him's language, which he understands in spite of its grammar mistakes and lexical peculiarities, Charles discovers that his illustrated dictionary is of no use to him when attempting to explain the nature of his disquieting situation and the inconspicuous threat that his parents' employee represents. This situation effectively illustrates the need to read between the lines in the novel where the performative quality of words does not necessarily mean that silence is the equivalent to inaction.

We also see this when he asks on three different occasions over the course of the novel: "How can you know or tell?" While soliciting the reader's help here, this question betrays Charles' feelings of bewilderment with respect to his pursuer's behaviour and shows that he is simply stuck, that is to say, caught between the end of childhood and the beginning of adolescence. Although he understands the sinister nature of the farmhand's innuendos and the inappropriateness of his behaviour toward him, Charles seems to overlook the fact that there is a physical difference between *him* and *Him*. During the confrontation in the barn where the boy fails to fully heed Him's advice to watch his back, he realizes too late that, no matter which way he turns, he is alone and vulnerable, just like the bay mare.

In the novel, the repeated mention of summer and the changing of the seasons foreshadows the arrival of the "Fall" or Charles' loss of innocence. Associated with school vacations, this time of the year alludes to the boy's forlorn feelings as he is stalked and then finally attacked. Abandoned by his family and the teachers, Charles lacks the know-how to deal with the antagonist who inundates him with words and a logic that he cannot quite grasp. Like the U.S. sergeant moving up the river, the farmhand progressively inhabits Charles to the point where he literally embodies him. Ironically, Charles describes this experience in terms of a void and someone having searched within his body. Robbed of his innocence, he is tormented by the lack of proof on his body, which bears no visible trace of the attack, and then, the change in his voice, which now resembles that of an adolescent. Brutally and prematurely initiated into this awkward time of life, Charles is disturbed by this unforeseen change which, despite its fatal character, seemingly provides him with a new voice; one that finally allows him to convey his experience in spite of his persistent silence in the denouement. By admitting at the end of the story that he is "Marlon

Brando," Charles recalls the actor's ashen face in the final scene of *Apocalypse Now* and effectively succeeds in bearing witness to the "horror" of his experience.

The theme of witnessing is an important notion when attempting to decipher the work's greater meaning and understand its form. Referring etymologically to a "third person standing by," the word "testimony" would seem to describe Charles' situation and his narrative, which effectively attests to an occurrence that history has not yet recorded. Indeed, the text's unnamed chapters, its oral characteristics and its resemblance to both a diary and a confession, recall this distinct and widely recognized literary genre that is often associated with Holocaust and war crime survivors. While one cannot compare Charles to such individuals, the novel's background provides context for the boy's remarks concerning the witness, who is the most important agent in any dramatic event in his opinion. Using this term when speaking about his father, Charles' remarks take on true significance when he subsequently assumes the position of the bay mare that he watched being abused by Him. Indeed, there are a chain of witnesses in the novel, including the reader who passively observes the tragedy as it unfolds. Unable to speak to Charles and inform him of the imminent danger he faces, the reader experiences the boy's powerlessness while at the same time acting as an accomplice to Him. Although we do not want to see any harm come to the boy, we, nonetheless, await the conclusion. This situation testifies to the unsettling but provocative nature of the story that describes an experience, which is not only Charles', but a recurring social phenomenon that we have only recently begun to overtly acknowledge and include in our collective memory.

Constructed in layers, the novel may depict an isolated personal incident on a farm somewhere in Quebec, but would seem to speak on behalf of all those silenced or without a voice. As such, the text lends itself to in-depth and allegorical readings. Having already been examined in terms of the literary institution and then a political allegory of Quebec's identity by certain critics, the novel would also appear to contain a subtext, which questions the Church's haunting presence in French-speaking Canada. Much like Jesus, Charles is a scapegoat of sorts insofar as he, too, is forsaken by his Father, although his resurrection at the end of the novel is nothing more than speculative. Albeit implicit, this biblical allusion would seem to be one of many in the novel, which inevitably makes the reader think about the numerous sex scandals involving religious institutions and the fact that Marlon Brando's character in *The Godfather* is also the head of the Mafia.

Seemingly rich in intertextuality, the novel is clearly thought-provoking and engaging, if nothing else. Dealing with topics such as betrayal, abandonment, the father figure, regret and coming-of-age, the novel also alludes to the increasingly important issue of bullying in our society. When considering the farmhand's behaviour, we see the insidious role that blackmail plays in this widespread phenomenon, which still plagues school-aged children today. Bigger, less intelligent, but more conniving, Him may very well be troubled by sentiments of guilt, but does not stop pursuing Charles in a bull-like fashion, before finally seeing red, as it were, in the barn where the diluvial rain imprisons the boy. Penetrating the shelter by means of a hole in the roof, the rain would appear to represent a flooding of sorts and the beginning of the end for the boy's childhood.

While *The Death of Marlon Brando* may tell a disturbing story, it is one well worth reading as it teaches us about the truly apocalyptic nature of child abuse and the need to listen to what people, and more importantly children, are *not* saying. By teasing out the sense of anticipation created by the title, the novel shows that there is, indeed, a sound to silence and that in order to fully understand, one must also interpret, infer and, even at times, translate. Tactfully crafted, Gobeil's novel plunges readers into a troubling and ambiguous world, which forces them to remain open to what is difficult to explain and appreciate. In this way, it proves that literature is much more than another form of entertainment; it is often the means by which people truly comprehend those "things" that simply cannot be expressed, or that facts are just unable to convey effectively.

As the translator of Pierre Gobeil's gripping and multifaceted text, I hope to have done it and its author justice. May this regrettably overlooked novel with the strange but intriguing title finally receive the recognition it deserves.

He calls this contraption an ornithopter. I thought he made up the word but I looked it up in a dictionary and it was there. It said an ornithopter was any aircraft designed to derive its chief support and propulsion from flapping wings. Who'd believe it? There's a word for everything.

—WILLIAM WHARTON, *Birdy*

The Death
of
Marlon Brando

He said: "The mare is gonna have its colt"...and me, I asked: "When?" He said that he didn't really know.

He said: "In a week, maybe...or a li'l bit before. It's hard to say like this, but the mare is pretty pregnant. It might be soon."

He said: "Do ya know where li'l colts come from? No, ya dunno..." and then he added: "Before we get to see them, I mean."

I turned my head and then let myself fall into the hay. That's just him! Ask a question and then answer it, right after. Colts, they come from mothers and fathers. A mare can have a little one each year, generally in the springtime, in March or April. Sometimes later, but most often in the spring. They come from fathers and mothers. It takes time, you have to wait...and even then, what does it matter, anyway? In my *Petit Larousse Illustré* dictionary, they show four words for "mare," whereas for "colt," they only give one... and this, without any other kind of explanation.

I didn't want to start up a conversation and so I didn't answer. I was up, and let myself fall again into the hay. And if there's something that I like doing, that's it, letting myself fall into the void: like that, diving or falling backwards. From the main beam, you can jump into the pile that's twenty feet below. For me, it's high up. There's a risk of getting hurt and it's a game.

He said: "Ya can't know, can ya..." and I didn't say anything back as sometimes I happen to not answer right away. I could have said: "We learned that at school" or "I've read a thousand books" or even "I've been living on a farm for so long that..." but I didn't say anything. I just let him work away because if he's at our place, it's to work. And I've noticed that the more things go on in this way, the more he wastes time.

Sometimes, just like that, I could say things and I keep quiet.

I could have also said: "We saw a film." I could've said: "There are ten thousand movies about it..." but I didn't.

Where was I? Sometimes, for reasons beyond me, I leave things up in the air and say nothing. And, I realize this more and more often now that I'm working on a composition structured like a war movie. It's as if, and truly as if, in order to really fight, I was at a loss for words.

Him, he was rubbing down the canisters and the wash buckets that had been used in the morning to do the milking. He was muttering, rehashing what has always seemed to me to be the same thing, and so I didn't listen to him. Sometimes, too, for no reason at all, I'd take off running in order to take refuge in the house or elsewhere. To flee for glee and because it's a game; because it's crazy what you can find in terms of hiding spaces and dark corners on a farm. You can even lie flat out in the bed of a Ford pickup and you're sure not to be seen. Him, too, he hides there sometimes and I've noticed that he's the only big person that I know who takes pleasure in acting like a child. Like borrowing your clothes, like chewing on candies, like laughing while trying to hide it, all of which are children's habits. And yet, I don't say this out loud. I'm writing a composition, as fine as the film that I like. I put forward facts, but they always seem to get covered up by beasts that I invent and that are as fabulous as an *Ornithorhynchus anatinus*. I'm unable to speak, you could say. Not any more, in any case. In my composition, I try to explain just like in *Apocalypse Now* what I've been able to observe up until now, but it's not working. I just go round in circles. As for Him, he's watching me. And I don't know how long it's going to last.

Just now, he was washing out the milker and making sure to not leave any dirt in the nipples because moss and the like can grow there. We'd asked him to watch out for this and he'd listened carefully, as he's docile in front of people. He was touching the machine with care as if it were a precious object. As for me, I was perched on the main beam and kept watching him work away at it in front of the door in the sun. He was rubbing hard, that's for sure, because my father had requested that he do so. And, in front of others, in front of my father, my mother and everyone in the house, he's obedient and tries to blend in.

Furthermore, I've noticed that with the others, he doesn't talk. He behaves; he makes grammar mistakes. You could say that he's ashamed, and because of this, he doesn't want to speak much with them, unless it's to say *oui* or *carrect* in order to say okay or yes sir. Just like the model employee that he wants to be, but he's not fooling anyone. And this causes him to make mistakes and stutter.

For example, he says *couchette, bacul* and *caltron*.[1] To say *courir* (to run), he says *runner*, as if it were a verb. He uses all kinds of French words and pretends that he's super-duper, but he isn't, really. In the beginning, the others would laugh when he said *carrect*. Not now. I'll admit here that I'm the only one who appears to be surprised by this. However, I don't speak. And so, correct or *carrect*, what does it matter?

Again. What power does a child have when he says that someone's too good? I think that he has none at all. At best, the child can trigger laughter and compliments about his wit for his age. At best, he can raise suspicions, but that people are quick to dismiss. What's for sure is that the others around me don't care to know any more than they need to. It would be too complicated, I think, or too much work. No time… It would be long and complicated and so they don't bother.

Furthermore, there's a ready-made answer for these types of things. It's an invented answer so that what I call "silencing"[2] reigns above all else. And this has happened since the beginning. I just know it. They're going to say: "You spend all your time watching things…" and they then add, before saying: "I gotta get going" which is a key phrase:

6

"Have ya replaced your pillow with a dictionary?"…and it won't go any further then. At our place, everyone pretends it's funny when I ask questions.

I'd have liked to name it, but it didn't work out. I've already tried to tell the whole story in my school composition; at home, too, that's just the way it is. But I don't have the words and so there's nothing doing.

The thing to do, just like today, is to let myself fall into the hay while he works away. Like this, diving or falling backwards. From the main beam, you jump into the pile twenty feet below. It's dangerous. For me, it's high up. There's a risk of getting hurt and it's a game.

If I don't speak, I've just explained the reason why. It seems to me that speaking doesn't serve any purpose. What's more, I think that speaking is the faculty of those who have nothing to say. "Silencing" comes from the verb "to silence," and to this day, I have described the beast watching the wanderer and yet, nothing has happened.

The other one was rubbing, swearing, singing tunes that he didn't finish. I was sitting on the beam and I was watching him do it. I like staying still. I like watching others work at times. In this way, I think that you can figure out what's going on in their heads. He was about to act up. He was about to do it; it was a sure thing, and he said:

"Hey, thingamajig…"

I waited. He said:

"Got any li'l girls in yer class?"…then he answered his own question: "Yeah there's some. I knew it."

I can guess where this is going. And as far as knowing whether someone is going to act up or not, I'm an expert. A clue? He always laughs a little bit just before. As if he were preparing the sentence in his head. He said: "Got any li'l girls in yer class?" I said: "Why?"…and he repeated his question once again.

I said: "What class are you talking about? Last year's or next year's?" I change classes once a year. Between the two, there's a long composition: it's my vacation assignment. "I don't know yet if there'll be any girls in September…but yeah. I think so."

He said: "Ya like that, huh?"…and he was laughing and hiding behind his hand.

I said: "What?" He didn't answer. He was laughing, covering up his mouth with his hand and making a racket while dragging his feet on the ground and moving his arms, too. In order to keep himself company no doubt; because he was used to laughing by himself and because I wasn't laughing.

I jumped into the hay and I brushed myself off. There were thorns stuck in my sweater and I pulled them out, one by one. After, I walked to the garden to see if the carrots and the apples had grown any since yesterday. To get some air and calm down, too, because being with him makes me get all flustered. I don't know why. And faced with this heart-beat that I don't have words for, I end up asking myself a question: Will I feel something similar later? Or more simply: Do risks exist for big people, too? I don't know. Today, I don't think so. I'm structuring my summer vacation assignment like a war film. I walk towards the garden, which is behind our house and which, because of its geographical location no doubt, is reassuring or worrisome. It depends.

A U.S. sergeant is going up the river in order to kill the colonel that Marlon Brando is playing. I make him the monster of my story.

And in my composition, I write:

The Ornithorhynchus is going up the river. But not in a canoe. It's a monster that sweats, that smells badly and that hides. The monster's odour bothers me. The beast makes itself look like a piece of wood. And the Abandoner and the Shadows don't exist yet.

I sat like a good little boy and was trying with the tip of my fingers to pull out the carrots that were ready to be eaten when he arrived behind my back. I'm not sure which, the surprise or the push, made me fall forward and crush several of them. I forgot about all that. Like a spring extending itself, my body slid out onto the vegetables. And right away, I thought of a fish. It was as if I'd run right into the glass walls of my bowl. He was there, now.

Hypocritically, he'd shown up from behind my back and had slid his hand under my heels and my thighs. It didn't hurt, but I was surprised at first. He said:

"The li'l girls are gonna do that at school." I didn't say anything back. I wanted to say "no" and that they would never let themselves do things like that...but my tongue stayed stuck on my front palate and I sputtered something that didn't mean anything. I tried to say that it was stupid, that nothing like that ever happened at our school ...I couldn't find the words; or rather yes, but these words didn't want to come out. And after a few attempts, which all failed, I kept quiet. Knowing very well that when the words don't come out, there's nothing you can do about it.

It was Saturday before noon and it was beautiful outside. The temperature was like that in lands far from the sea, a little dry, quite hot...still the month of August. He crouched down and started looking for carrots that were ready to be eaten.

He's the only big person that I know who does things that kids would think of doing. Suddenly, he starts looking for bigger and bigger buds, like you were doing a little while

11

ago. And if it were not him, if it were not this innocent person who speaks poorly, who makes noises when eating and who spits on the ground, you could say to yourself while watching him that what you were doing just before was the most fabulous thing imaginable. For him, you're a genius. The others say that he's different; me, I've concluded that he follows children because he finds them weak and that he's able to reason with them, as he's lacking this faculty himself. There's never been any doctor's note on this. They find him funny. Me, I think he's a beast. And I think that being a beast isn't exactly funny. He's a real beast who says dirty things; with whiskers, claws and false teeth. In some ways, he's stayed a child still, too. And, it's easy to see that he doesn't like to just play with them and that he doesn't like to just speak with them, as if, and exactly as if, the adults were in another world, separate from his. He thinks that he's part of the animals' and children's world, that's for sure. His words, his relationship with words, that's where he trips up and loses his place… And, all things considered, it's got to be a bit like a baby learning to walk. Like a one-year-old. The difference being that him, if he falls, he falls on others. And you, you're the one that he's going to wipe his bloodied mouth all over.

When I went to see the apples on the old apple trees, I knew that he'd come. I saw him from beneath the tree branches walking between the vegetable furrows, making as if he was interested in the carrots that were big enough to eat, acting as only he knows how to act sometimes. As for me, I knew that he'd come towards the apple trees and sure enough, he came. He's a pest, like a termite or louse that doesn't let you go. He likes following you and staying close to you. He doesn't go to the city and everyone is always surprised to see that he has his own opinions, despite everything.

"Do ya study the catechism?"...is what he asked me.

Had to hear the sound of the letters. T...T...T...Phew! It seemed like a lot. The word catechism, too. For sure, my teacher at school from last year didn't pronounce it like that. In a word that according to her had four syllables, he made it only two by emphasizing in a big way the first "t." You could say that he takes certain liberties with words. His first syllable is exactly like the word "cat" in English. He asked me whether we studied the catechism and I said yes. I said that we had bible study at school and, as usual, I'm sure that I told him something that he already knew. He's like that. He always asks the same questions and doesn't want to let you get on your way. Because he's got a goal, that's for sure. And holding you back is one of his goals, I think. So, I said:

"Yes, we study the catechism at school and it's even one of the first subjects of the day. It's part of almost every morning of any given week. We have our morality lesson for half an hour just before recess, which is before more practical subjects. Math, for example. However, one morning a week, we've got history and then another, geography."

He said: "Ya heard of the story of Adam an' Eve an' the apple tree. Have ya?…"

"Have ya…Have ya, huh, huh…?" Phew, again… With each answer, he took the liberty of taking a bite of an apple and making a little screeching noise. The overflowing juice of the apple seemed to him to be like an affirmative answer and so he kept on going. Even if he doesn't wipe his mouth and has a body that seems to sway when he puts on his boots, you can be sure that he knows how to make connections. Under the apple trees, he rehashes the story of Adam and Eve. Well done. As I was telling him about how subtle he was, he said:

"It ain't true, this story. It's not true that Eve bit into an apple. All that's a lyin'."

He knows how to make connections, that's for sure. In his head, there is a whole series of old stories that he's learned, I don't know from where, and that he brings up from time to time when he's alone with me. Most often, it's the same stories and I think that he knows them by heart. I could've sworn that he was going to say: "It ain't true what they tell ya at school"…and then he said:

"It ain't true what they're tellin' ya at school." After, he added: "It's all a lyin'. They're takin' ya for dummies. Me, I hardly even went to school in Ontario, an' I know more than you all. Eve didn't bite into an apple. Eve bit here, there." He laughed and covered his mouth with his hand. He looked around in order to see if anybody was coming. After, he spat on the ground and then put his foot on it.

What's he going to come up with next? Before, he con-
tented himself with words and now he's going at it full
force. Maybe he's simply making fun of me? Maybe it's
because I'm young that he's overdoing it? I left and went
into the house where I knew that he could follow me, but
where I also knew that he'd have to change topics.

For some time now, I've noticed that he isn't quite the same
when there are people around. He says very little or nothing
at all; he does favours and never, unless it's absolutely necessary, deals with me directly. It's weird. It's like a game. I've
noticed that he acts as if I don't exist in front of the others.
He, who when we're alone, is always ready to ask questions
and tell stories – I've often told him that he'd go to prison
and I really believe it – but with others, he's someone else.
Almost good or indifferent. If he needs somebody to pass
him the salt when he's at the table, he'll always ask someone else.

In the kitchen, my mother said: "Your father's gone. You
look like you're bored. Tomorrow, you can go into town with
him. In the meantime, come help me fill the little cakes.
You can eat some."

So I sat down without saying anything and I began to cut
up the small balls of dough, which were still warm, into
equal parts. On the radio they were saying that in California
they had discovered a network of child-slaves brought in
from Mexico. They put people in prison and other prisoners

beat them. Because they had done things like that to children...And I thought that they were using me in this house, too. And she added:

"When you're done, you can go help him put the milk canisters on the small table. It's going to be time for the truck in a little while. He likes it better when you go with him."

In my composition, with the help of a war film, I reinvent all the words that I can't say. But because it's only a child's story, it isn't taken seriously. It's complicated. The film is long, and in my own story, everything has to happen in a weekend.

Moreover, in my composition, I don't dare write simple sentences because they say too much. I don't dare write sentences like this one:

He's watching me. Well, I think that he's watching me...as he looks at me and if I surprise him, he quickly turns his head. "To lie in wait," and in my dictionary for this expression, it says: lie in wait for the enemy. As if there were a struggle, and as if somewhere, punches had been thrown that you can count.

In my composition, word after word, sentence upon sentence and hidden by a fantastic story, I try to tell what's happening to me in real life. It's funny. You'd say that I want to speak, but at the same time that I'm afraid of being understood. I invent. I redistribute roles and I break down the plots. In the film, there's a sergeant gone on a mission to kill the American colonel. Washington approves and the others are indifferent. In my composition, there's the Ornithorhynchus, the Abandoner and the Shadows. In that order.

It's hunting time. It's the jungle and there's a river. And, in my story, the Ornithorhynchus is watching the wanderer.

After dinner, I was given several tasks to do and I kept busy the whole time. It's always like that on the farm. I know, as I'm used to it. There's always something to do, someone to help out, a message to pass along…and when you are a child, they use you for things like that. So much so that I haven't had time to read; my *Petit Illustré* dictionary stayed on the little table the whole day. I ran the whole afternoon and if the sun, which was beating down on the railway, made me think of summer, I knew that this really wasn't the case anymore.

The trails and the undergrowth were still moist and fresh like they'll be until winter. And there's a bitter odour that sticks to the earth and tries to make itself known. The sweet languishing of summer is followed and replaced by an indescribable taste of dead leaves, bark and brush. I don't know why the seasons exist. And I don't know why, already at the end of August, you can smell these smells even though they're not real for another few weeks yet. In my dictionary, there's no word to describe this experience.

The days go by slowly and the season remains so uncertain that you no longer know who you can trust.

In the afternoon, when I came back to *Timothy-en-bas* after having gone to get some string, the others had left and he was all alone in the barn. When he saw me, he began walking in circles, glancing up at me and laughing. He was going to act up, I knew it. He said:

"They're gonna come back. They left ya here to change the tractor battery because it was startin' to skip. They didn't want ya gettin' in the way while they were workin'. Once it's started, you gotta finish. Without that, we get all cruddy. The combine is *ready*. They said that ya had no business with 'em. They said that they hadda get goin'. Go get some water with the pail."

I sat down just beneath a hole in the roof, made by a tile that had been ripped off by the wind. The sun had halted there and the dust from the fields, full of mounds of oats, was being stirred up. Canadian geese, fifteen or so, squawked on the way by, and a sentence came to mind: "It's the end, he said"...like that, for nothing and not too loudly, for me, without speaking for any real reason. To say nothing and maybe because it's a game. All that came to me from a book.

At school last year, before the June vacation, I mean, our teacher read us a novel that was written by a woman who lived on a riverbank. Upon seeing geese go by, a man said: "It's the end." In the story, he was clearly only saying "it's the end," but for me, in my head, I recorded the words of the book. So much so that now when I see wild geese going by, I say this sentence: "It's the end, he said." This shows that the words are not mine, but from this man called Didace. It shows clearly that the sentence came from the story, which is not mine, but that of a woman who lived on the banks of a river.[3]

Him, he said: "It's a pack goin' south with the li'l ones"…and he said again: "But, how old are ya, again?"

And I wondered if my age had anything to do with these birds and their hatchlings.

The geese, the first of the season, were flying overhead like an arrow just over the opening in the roof. When they got to the height of the sun, I lost them. Because of the sunlight, no doubt, which is brilliant, yellow and lively, forcing you to squint. Because of the distance perhaps, as the geese go far. And to do this, they have to fly high up. I rolled over, stretched out my whole body by putting my neck back, and my heart raced… But it was for nothing, as once the geese were gone, I was still the same.

I'm a little skittish and seeing the geese fly by and flee towards the south worries me. In the summer on the farm, you don't see many people and those that are around take up all the space.

Sometimes, because of signs like the geese, I become aware of my fear, which must be just like Marlon Brando's waiting for the U.S. sergeant. But not always, however. Most often, fear is deaf or invisible or hidden, and my hands stay in my pockets as if nothing was happening. Most often when I think about it, I forget. The most visible failure is words. I forget, I try to forget, I mean. Then, I continue my day like everyone continues their day: I get up and I walk.

I sat up, took the pail, and went down to the spring, the source located several feet below the earth cut into big steps that we call *Tim-en-bas*. For this reason, we say that it's hidden. Our spring goes to the bottom of the ravine, secret and fresh, and I think that it doesn't like being bothered. Maybe this is why it's capricious and that my father thinks it won't flow anymore before long.

Already in July, my father once said: "The spring is dried up." I asked: "What does that mean, dried up."[4] Father said: "It's when you don't have any more. It's when it's finished" and, for us, that was a bad thing, really.

Sure that in my *Petit Illustré* dictionary, there's no picture to accompany this word. But it's there, you can be sure of that. And I think that this alone is all the proof we need so as to keep an eye out.

During those hottest of times in summer, I think that it's the spring which makes our fields worth something and I know that our father admires it. It's necessary, and he once said to me, while squinting his eyes: "It's precious and, for that reason, it's hidden at the bottom of the ravine."

He thought that he got me with his little stories for children between four and eight years old, but I said to him: "That's a sentence taken right out of a fairy tale" and he laughed. After, he said: "You talk like in your books." Then he turned away, shrugged his shoulders and opened his hands. And sometimes, because of nothing, or because of little things like that, like the shoulders, the words, the hands, I've got the distinct impression that my father hasn't noticed that I've grown up.

When I was at the bottom of the ravine and had hollowed out a cavity that was big enough in order to fill my pitcher, I could sense that he was behind me. I have to say that the more things seem to be alright, the more I think that he's always behind me. I also have to say that the more things are fine, the more I have trouble finding the words capable of expressing the panic I feel when faced with the threat.

The first thing that I heard were the branches rustling. After that, his shadow emerged over the short stretch of black and freezing water. I turned around and he said, while laughing a little and being a little embarrassed, too, and covering his mouth with his hand like he always does, "As for me, I'm with thirst." Then he added, "Them snow gooses, ain't interestin'." He didn't need anything else to believe that he'd been invited.

He got down on all fours and set about lapping up the liquid like an animal would have done. We weren't at the table, that's true, but that suction noise and the drooling seemed intolerable. You could easily see that as far as quenching his thirst was concerned, there was as much water falling out as was going in. So much so that, after a certain amount of time, he was drinking the water that had just fallen into the small dugout I'd made. It was nothing less than horrible to see all this. I pushed through the branches and went back up the steep path in order to wait for the others. Without knowing why, for no reason whatsoever no doubt, my heart was pounding. Like a little while ago, with the sun on the dry earth of the trail.

And to say that my father's land is beautiful regardless of the season, and this even during the winter when it's all covered in snow, I'm not so sure now, and sometimes I even forget this. It's undulating, with no rocks, moist and rich. They say that it's one of those plots of land, maybe they should say soils, that are the most fertile in the region. My father says this and, personally, I believe him.

And I enjoy thinking about things like that when I walk with my hands in my pockets, alone, without any friends. I like imagining that our land is a domain, which arouses admiration and fear everywhere around here. I wanted to say this, but my father says that when you're walking in the fields, out of respect for the land itself, you shouldn't speak. I found that funny at the beginning, but now I stay silent in order to act properly.

In this way, when I end up walking with him, we don't speak. When I end up walking with my father, we never walk side by side. He goes in front, and me, I follow him. Once, I even imagined that if I stopped walking, he'd continue on his way.

They can't prevent me, however, from seeing what's around me. The others, I know them. I know that they're older than me and that they don't really exist. In my story, they're the Shadows and, in order to fight back, they call me the Cake Eater. Our relationship, for me and them, is limited to these quality-control labels.

Him, I observe more closely than the others. Sometimes, even, I examine him – his head, round; his hands, webbed – and in front of the Shadows, I know that he's elusive; he hides and doesn't say anything. You never see his eyes. As for his hands, when I let myself go and describe them in my composition where I invent scenes from things that I know, they're paws with fingers stuck to one another …like those of a duck. In June, when making up my plan, I had to describe the Ornithorhynchus in my story and he's the one I saw right away. It's bizarre, and when the teacher asked me jokingly if I had already seen a platypus, I said yes. After, I changed my mind, but it was too late and my teacher, who has eagle eyes under her horn-rimmed glasses, said:

"So you've already seen a platypus, have you?" Our teacher from last year used to speak to say nothing. She asks me this type of question even though she knows full well that I've never seen one. A caricature of a schoolteacher if you want to know; hair in a bun, white blouse, a cameo…

I know that I could have continued to answer yes, but I also know that my cause would have been difficult to defend. So, I asked to go wash my hands.

I said: "I stained my hands with oil from my bicycle chain. Can I go to the bathroom?"

She accepted. This is what she does when she doesn't refuse. You'll understand: never is she going to say yes or no. She refuses or she accepts. She teaches. A caricature, I told you. Her only initiative has been to give us an assignment for the month of June that lasts the whole summer. A revolutionary! I have to say that I enjoy applying myself to compositions and that I like words. I also have to say that as the revolution would have it, she gave us a trick. She said:

"Take a subject that's close to you...something that you know. In order to help you, think about the structure of a story that you've already read or seen somewhere. On T.V.; at the movies or elsewhere. She added: "It always works..."

I chose a film on Vietnam. Because knowing that it was Washington that abandoned the American colonel, that really struck me.

While rubbing my hands under the hot water faucet using the liquid soap – at school, we have liquid soap like for kitchen dishes and I like it – I thought that I could have invented another story. Say that because of a sticky candy, speak about the mud because it's raining outside...I could have even said: "May I go to the bathroom?" but I didn't. No matter, now. All I needed was for it to get me out this platypus business that I'd seen, but that I couldn't explain. I succeeded. For a while, in any case. And so here's what I've become: the specialist at inventing stories. Once again you'll understand; I could even have said: "May I go to the bathroom?"...as I know how to conjugate the verb "to be able" in this way.[5] But, I didn't do it. In general, I keep quiet. More and more, my uneasiness makes me act like the platypus – Him – the one who wiggles his webbed feet in front of others, rolls his eyes that are difficult to describe, but doesn't speak.

When he does, he also uses strange words and expressions that sound funny. At first, the others used to laugh, but today, you'd say that I'm the only one who appears surprised by this. He says things like *couchette* and after a while you notice that he is talking about *fourchette* (fork), the kitchen utensil. He says: *candies*. And I know that for him, that means *sweets*. As if, and just as if, all the candies were made of sugar candy. He even manages to make up sentences like this one. He says, for example: "the chicken there…" Swear that I'm not making up a thing. He says: "The chicken there…" and I think it means "*That* chicken there," or the chicken that we have right in front of us. It's unbelievable. A three-year-old knows fewer words, but I'm sure that his sentences are better constructed than the ones that the monster would call "his to himself." I truly believe that. I owe it to myself to also say that he doesn't speak very much to men, that he mostly blabs away to himself or speaks to the animals.

My mother says that he drinks and that he's developed their habits by spending so much time with them. She doesn't say anything else about it. I also have to say that since he doesn't speak much to others, the others don't speak much about him. I've noticed that, too. In front of them, in front of my father, my mother and even in front of the people at the house, he's obedient. In general, he listens well – too well, perhaps. And, I suspect him of hiding something, but how do you tell someone this – and try to do them a favour? Them, most often, they just ignore him as they think that this is the way it should be. And him, he takes advantage of being ignored in order to sneak about.

Once again: to say *noyer* (drown), he says the word *neyer*. And with *neyer*, it's like there's already water flowing in his throat. That one there, he uses onomatopoeias without even knowing it. He says *neyer*, becomes sad and tries to make you feel for him. Without knowing it either, he's an Ornithorhynchus who invents words – *zezon, petuite, jouquer*,[6] uses *neyer* once again because he feels guilty. And sometimes I wonder if his power doesn't reside in something like this. Sometimes in the evening, I think about it, especially when I'm alone; after something bad has happened, often… Like this night when our dog got hit by a car. You'd say that I only think about it when I'm sore. And so it's too late, and for the most part, all my energy is spent. In my dreams at night, I often see myself putting out a fire with my boots like we do in the fields of grass. And the fire continues, spreads and ravages everything.

When I saw *Apocalypse Now*, I thought of that, too. A war movie!... The finest there is! And I decided to construct my story like this movie that I love.

It was only later on that the others came by. They'd changed the tractor's battery, had brought some fruit and, for me, Mom had put in a little cake. This was in August. The last days of August are short. At around six o'clock in the evening when I said that I wanted to walk home, he said that he would go back to the house on foot, too. Right away, I felt trapped. I said no; that I wanted to go down alone and that he had no business following me. My father said "Tut-tut..." I said: "Can I not get any peace around here?" My father said "Tut-tut..." I said: "This is unjust." He looked at me, taken aback. You'll understand: when I pronounce the word injustice, for my father, it's as if I were saying *onhuebbtr mnjssterr,* or even *llksiuytyyty.*

In short, it's as if, and just as if, in his dictionary, the one he uses, this word wasn't there.

I set off on the dirt road which is cracked and dry. It undulates and is serpentine, and is beautiful or ugly; it depends. Him, he went the same way no doubt, but I was walking quickly and didn't turn around.

I had already written: "The monster's odour puts me off..." but he was one I wanted to name.

There was the meal and I thought that we were still there in front of a summer dinner. Because of the squash soup and salads, because of the corn on the cob too, which were reigning over the table like beautiful bright yellow marbles, and also because of the raspberries for the dessert. In summer, the salads are made up of lettuce and Mom leaves the bottles of oil on the table for us to season them ourselves.

There were the doors that open out onto the warm evening and twilight came about at eight o'clock, I believe. There hadn't been any mosquitoes for more than a month, but all the leaves were still on the trees. You knew that the summer was coming to an end, but never would you have dared say that autumn was near. That's the way it is with the seasons. You feel them long before talking about them for real.

Father sat down on the veranda as he so often does, cleared his throat, smoked his pipe, cleared his throat once again and went inside to go to bed. This was earlier than near the beginning of June, it would seem. Earlier, because the days were getting shorter, perhaps. My mom was watching the T.V.

There were the boys and the girls, all brothers and sisters, and you could hear them getting ready. They were in one room that we call the addition[7] and you couldn't see them, as they're the Shadows. Them, they're living, laughing, and are at an age where you only look after yourself. They dance, laugh, work, but do nothing else and, in my

33

story, it's as if they weren't there. They go out. In the house, there's only Father, Mother and Him who pay attention to me. For the Shadows, my composition is nothing other than a fantasy of the Cake Eater. Also, I wander around all alone for the most part in the courtyard, on the farm…and then on the whole property. In the clouds, on the roads and in books.

I went to the paddock of the *Grande Montée* to see if the bulls had been given anything to drink. I do this in the evening even if for the most part, they've already had something to drink. Father wants me to check on the state of the reservoir every day. It's always different. It isn't very far away, and on the hill there's always a bit of wind. Evenings are cool there and it's comfortable.

When I got close to the reservoir to which we'd attached a drainage valve, I saw that he was there. He was coming out from behind the trees and didn't look at me. In fact, I think that he was pretending to be there by chance, and when he finally made up his mind to look at me he made as if he was surprised. He said: "Ha…" and me, I made as if I wasn't duped by being surprised. It was the right thing to do. He laughed to himself and said:

"Yer father sent me to clean the reservoir…" Then he started walking around it while covering his mouth with his hand and dragging his feet, too. He also grabbed his nose with his hand and even went so far as to pull on it in the shadow of the leaves. I thought that this was an abhorrent gesture.

It's still summer. I see it in the bunches of cherries, hanging heavily from the tree branches like when we used to bale the hay. We used to grab handfuls of them in order to stuff our faces.

It's still summer because of the wind or the air and its weather patterns, which I don't understand. It must be a complicated system whereby the air goes from high to low and across in arches, then whirls and twirls and advances softly like a caress. This is something that in three weeks will no longer exist, for example, and that won't come back until ten months from now with the new summer.

In my composition, I already wrote about the summer, that we're always waiting for it.

It's still daytime or evening-daytime and from above, I can see the houses camped in the valley, all surrounded by apple trees, agricultural equipment and vehicles. Behind each house, you can see a vegetable garden. In front of all the houses is a lawn, which changes from the surrounding meadows due to its colour, due to it being a bald patch, due to its odour. I can't see them from here, so I invent them.

He said: "Ya must be lookin' forward to returnin' to school, huh, thingamajig? It must be pleasant to go to school. Ya must be happy…" and I answered no.

He said: "If yer lookin' forward to goin' to school, it's gotta be because of the girls." He said: "Ya like that, thinkin' about the girls, huh?…" and as I didn't answer, because he was acting like such a know-it-all, and due to my answer which couldn't be either a yes or a no, he kept on saying: "Ya gotta do things with the girls durin' recess."

I was going to say to him that we didn't even see the girls during this time, that they're on the other side of the playground, when he said: "Don't pretend ya don't understand. Ya know more than yer lettin' on. I know what ya do durin' recess."

I said: "What are you rambling on about?" and for an instant, he didn't know what to think. I saw him clearly hesitate and then he said:

"Yer friend from the village is the one who told me things…Huh…huh Ya surprised, huh?… Ya didn't think that I was aware of what yer up to."

I certainly was surprised, but more by the fact that he knew Louis Levasseur than by what he might very well know about our recesses. What's he going to dig up next? What business is it of his anyway? And why exactly was he talking about "recesses" while emphasizing this word and making innuendos? So much so that I already felt guilty about something just by hearing him say "recesses." And that, even if in general, we only kicked the ball about during this time at school.

He said:

"Here now, yer thing, it's not even as big as that." And I understood, because it was easy to understand even when he mumbles and his speech is muddled. As for his images, they're always clear. What's more, with him, you always know beforehand what the conversation is going to be about. He was showing me the end of the barrel spout while laughing a little because it was embarrassing, even to him. He was also mixing up his words as he does when he's excited. He then added:

"Maybe at recess, ya show yer li'l thing to the girls. I know this now, ya know."

This whole episode didn't bother me in the slightest. I'm used to it with him. He's an Ornithorhynchus and he's dirty. With him, you already know beforehand what the conversation is going to be about. First, the mare and chicks, Eve and the apple, and then the birds and their brood. He knows how to make connections, I've already said this.

He continued: "Is it true that you'z guys had a dirty magazine last year? Huh… huh?… Ya not sayin' anythin' now," was what he said. "That, that's gotta be true. I'm informed, ya know."

I answered no, but it was true that we'd looked at it. I have to say that I was surprised to find out that he was aware of this. Once again, I was stunned to see that beneath his innocent exterior, there was some sort of intelligence at work. He knew about the magazine. It was true that this type of thing interested him and he knows how to be tenacious. He's a spy too, and with respect to this type of thing, with respect to digging into things, I mean, he's a pro. We found a magazine that was called *Baby*. We had hid it in our desks between our workbooks, buried it under our school manuals for weeks and he still knew about it.

How? I don't know. No doubt after having snooped about, kept an eye out and picked up bits of conversation that people exchanged. And because he's on the lookout, he knows everything about everybody and anyone, and he tells me this repeatedly while saying that I should watch my back. Be wary of others, for sure. If I were to believe everything he said, I should be afraid of everyone. Even of my friend Louis because he'd said while holding the photo in his hands that it must smell good. I remember that we laughed – we were together with Marc – the three of us, leaning against the school wall, hidden with our hands full of texts in English. We couldn't read them, and so we just imagined. We were saying to each other that one day we'd buy a car and we'd go to the United States. The end of our trip would be Texas. We'd already measured the distance between our village and the border, and already we'd found a used car that would go a hundred miles an hour at times.

All three of us were leaning up against the wall and were making plans: Texas!

As for the rest of the United States, it wasn't important...as I knew that over there, there were gas stations where you can get gas all night long.

He said: "Ya see full well that I'm informed. Huh...Yer not sayin' nothin'. Magazines of the sort where ya see everythin'. Me, I got some too. Photas in colour, I got some. Do ya wanna see them? Yer interested huh...? Ya pretend that ya don't bother with that, but yer interested in seein' the li'l girls. On the page in the middle, one of 'em is peein'. Ya jealous? Ya'd like to have a phota like that, wouldn't ya, huh…? Yer jealous of my colour photas. If yer good, I'll show ya some… Ya'll see. Beautiful photas. The one on the page in the middle, it folds out. If I had an apartment to me alone, I'd attach it above my bed…and in the evenin' I'd lay down underneath it. It'd be like havin' drops fall on my face."

He was acting like someone sleeping. He was opening his mouth and acting like he was snoring. He kept saying "phota" and I think that he spent ten minutes, not one less, stuck on this word, which, for goodness sake, is hardly difficult to pronounce: "photo."

He was saying: "I'll show ya…" and laughed all by himself like he often does, when he covers his mouth with his hand as if he doesn't want to show off his dentures. He was making fun as he sometimes does. He kept saying while laughing: "We all know, us, the bare truth, yer not interested in that stuff. Us, barely old enough…" and he kept on laughing and insisting on the bare of barely, which meant us, the three boys. I said:

"Stop sleeping and get your butt in gear if you don't want my father to show up and find the work not done. You spend your day dragging your heels. My father's going to clean your clock. Wait, you're going to see."

He was laughing to himself as he often does. With his hand in front and his false teeth behind. I turned around and went running down the hillside. At the bottom is the

farm; there are people there and things are happening.
People live down there.

The others, the boys and the girls of the house, go out on
Saturdays and other nights too, but most often on Saturday
evening, you'd have to say. I asked: "Why on Saturday?..."
and they said: "We don't know. The others go out on this
day, too, and we like it when there's lots of people."

Me, I said: "And why on Saturday?" They didn't know.
They said that for them, they like it when there are lots of
people. For him, it's the opposite, I think.

What's remarkable about him is that he doesn't go out
with the other boys and girls his own age. If Mother tells
him that he can leave for once, he shakes his head, groans
and says that he's tired. He manages to let the others leave
and stays there. What I understood right away was that
because of this situation, when the others go dancing,
Mother and Father go to bed early, us, we end up alone
together, him and me. I wanted to go read on the veranda,
but he said:

"Come an' play cards." He said: "Hey, do ya know that
one, the game of Queen of Spades?" He said: "I'm gonna get
the nu'deck of cards. There's Pepsi in the fridge. Wait...
we're gonna have some fun."

The others, they're Shadows. You know that they're there
or that they already have been there, but you don't know
much else about them. They cross the house and the farm,

a bit like the Abandoner does, and respond to laws that I haven't quite yet been able to understand. Like Saturday evening for example, they're not there. On Saturday night, they systematically abandon the one they call "The Cake Eater."

Me, the one who always finds cards boring, I must say that I like playing his game. It's so simple. You can learn to play it in less than two minutes and then it's smart. In fact, you pretend that it's smart because I'm of the opinion that chance does eighty percent of the work, and observation the rest. Nothing to do with intelligence in that case, then. This is what I believe. But him, seeing that I was winning regularly, he said: "Huh, so yer brilliant…"

He kept repeating "so yer brilliant…"

Once he said: "So yer handsome." I got up and finished my Pepsi in one gulp. That was the first time he'd said this.

The evening was mild, humid and, because of the clouds, night came quickly. We found ourselves together in the addition where it was still hot. The light, which was nothing other than a bulb suspended from a wire, was swinging when a breeze came in and dried the drops that were hanging from his nose.

He was drenched for no reason. We'd stopped playing. The radio had stayed on, but there was no music. It was a talking radio. Like him. I've already said that when he was with me, he never stopped talking. I can also say that his habit of talking to the animals had turned into long monologues that a listener isn't quite able to grasp. He kept saying:

"Hey, that there blue, it suits ya well. Is that there a new shirt? Where's it that ya got it? It's a nice blue. I'll have to get myself buyin' the same one."

He kept saying, too: "I dunno if it'd be too li'l for me. Do ya wanna let me try it?"

I already said that he was the only big person who would act like a child. He'd drink his Pepsi, make noises while swallowing and sometimes when laughing too much – he'd laugh all by himself. As for me, I wouldn't unclench my teeth as a thin web of cola and saliva trickled down his chin.

He said: "Tomorrow, if ya want, I gotta go get the bay mare. Would ya like that?" He said: "Would ya like that, to go horse ridin' for a long time? Let's go out the whole day…after we've set out the canisters."

"Tomorrow is Sunday," I said to him, "and we have to go to Church. After, I have something…"

He said: "Right away after dinner if ya want. We'll go up to *Clos-à-Julie*, then I'll brin' you the leather saddle. Yer father wants to have the mare down there because she's gonna foal pretty soon. Ya wanna? Say yes, right away."

I answered no, that tomorrow I'd go into town with my father. That we'd go right away after dinner and that we might get back late. In general, when my father goes to town, he isn't back before eight o'clock in the evening. I told him that we'd leave right away after mass and that if my mom didn't have the time to prepare a lunch for us, we'd go to a restaurant.

He said: "That ain't right at all. Because it ain't no spot for kids over there, an' then he ain't got the time to look after ya. Yer father, he won't wanna take ya over there. I'm sure a that." He continued:

"In the cities, it's dangerous for kids. Ya never know what could happen. Never in a hundred years. Ya should watch yer back."

He said: "We're gonna have another game of cards," then he added: "Never in a hundred years is yer father gonna wanna find himself stuck with a kid over there."

I said no and went outside onto the veranda first and then into the courtyard, and then onto the paved road and onto to the dirt trail that goes up to the top. It was night-time. You could figure out what season it was, although it was no longer one, by the sounds of the world more so than by the mild wind, the rustling breeze or the turmoil that I imagined was surrounding me.

It was no longer the summer and it wasn't yet autumn either. I didn't have a word that I could use to name this period. A dog was barking all alone. Flapping wings becoming sometimes no more than a simple whistle, and especially the noise of the air in the dry leaves. This all seemed to announce the end of a moment in time. In a few days it would be back to school, in a few months Christmas, and then, after the spring…then again, more summers.

Images were coming one after the other in a regular fashion, but slowly, like in the morning when, without warning, they'll start to jump on my toes. Like fingers on the keys of a piano.

And I could see myself getting old. I could see myself already grown-up. I already was, all things considered, since I'd walk during the night without asking for permission to do so. Wasn't this a privilege reserved for big people…along with having money in your pocket and the power to defend yourself?

How much time do I still have to wait? I was doing the calculation in my head. I was imagining myself in a few years travelling with a backpack filled with utensils, cards, compasses, and a whole bunch of different objects easy to carry and absolutely necessary to anyone looking to make it big. I wanted Texas. Because on the globe in his room, it's the second-biggest state in the whole of the United States. And, I like that it's far.

At night sometimes, because of nothing at all, I'd feel intoxicated. I used to dream of short-story picture books, of epic adventures and of quests; I would have liked to believe that everything and anything is possible. To be able to say anything and everything and tell all, for example. How long do I still have to wait? In my composition, I spoke about a beast that's spying on me. None of this has left me satisfied.

One time in my bed, I heard steps on the floor and I raised my head. He was there, in the door frame giving onto the hallway, and wasn't saying anything. I couldn't see his face because of the half-light coming in and he stayed still…but I knew that it was him. He didn't say anything maybe, I'm not sure. Perhaps I heard his breathing, which was shallow and as if he were tired. But, how can you tell or know? I'd lowered my head and after a few attempts to get to sleep, I said:

"What are you doing there?" I said: "You're not going to bed?" I said: "Are you crazy?…" and he didn't answer.

His body, which was still at first, started to swing slowly, regular-like, and was accompanied by breathing; this also slow and regular at first. Then it became quicker and staccato-like, falling in time and harmony with the movement of his body, which was leaning up against the door frame.

I said: "You dancing?"

I said: "You jiggin'?"… and, since he didn't respond, I lay back down again on my bed. Once again I tried to sleep, but it was difficult and I just couldn't. Knowing that he was there, him, standing there, without saying a word, and fidgeting, with his breathing getting heavier and heavier…

When I rolled over on my side, I heard a groan, not that loud but still surprising. And before I had the time to roll over to see what was happening, he'd disappeared into his room or elsewhere…I don't know. He'd disappeared and I slept. I can rest in that case, but I can't sleep when someone's watching me.

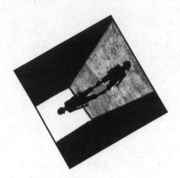

As for his origins, he said that he came from Ottawa, but we knew that he came from farther away; from French-speaking Ontario, is what my father knew. Meanwhile, my mother said: "…from over there…" My mother had said: "From the north?…" and my father responded: "No, from French-speaking Ontario, but from the south…" and then added before leaving: "As for the land, you can tell that he knows his stuff."

I'm talking here about the beginning. When he'd just arrived with his bags; when he was still nice, when he worked hard, without rambling on, and this even when he was all alone and I was there. I remember that in the spring my father and my brothers went to get him at the train station. When they got back, my father introduced me to him, as he was going to be "the hired man of the house" for a certain time.

My father had said:

"Him, he's the youngest of the boys, the one with his nose always in a book…" and the other one, the unknown farmhand, didn't say anything. It was like he didn't even look at me. He dragged his bags and I just noticed a glance from him that put me ill at ease. Because I was already fragile, and could already recognize a hypocritical look when I saw one.

During the first few days, he was mysterious. He had an accent and the neighbours wanted to come see the "stranger," hear him speak and find out what was new. He was different and seemed content to have the others take an interest in him.

Also, in his bags, he showed me an object that you wouldn't expect to find there: a golf umbrella. It was among his clothes, which were old and torn for the most part, that he'd brought from Windsor in Ontario or in Detroit, I don't really know – he kept saying Windsor and that he had relatives always *ready* in Windsor – a coloured umbrella that had come from the south, like something that had been lost.

And there was another thing in his bags. A globe of the earth, which he never used, and books that he never opened…but which pointed to the fact that he was not as innocent as he claimed to be, and that caught my attention from the start, whether I wanted it to or not.

During the first few days, his funny words, his unusual objects and his hardiness at work made it so that we liked him. My father kept saying: "As for the land, you can tell that he knows his stuff…" and, as for me, I was happy because my mother, who was asking questions about his origins, had said: "We're lucky to have stumbled on him."

It was like, in one sense, my mother had sensed the fall from her kitchen.

I woke up and realized it was Sunday. And at pretty much the same time, I thought that it was the last day of summer vacation and that it was the last few days of summer. Contrary to my routine, I stayed in bed for a long time without doing anything and without saying anything. I was lost in my thoughts, which I would certainly have trouble classifying. They weren't sad, okay, but they weren't exactly joyful, either. It would be difficult to name all of them and the right word to describe them perhaps doesn't even exist in my dictionary. What I can say about this is that they were coming to me regularly and slowly, one after another without trying to impose themselves and without trying to hang onto one another, either. I just let them go and watched my thoughts…but without being able to truly name them.

Then a ray of sunlight came in and stopped on the edge of my blanket. Suddenly, it caught fire, and suddenly, I was hot. It was truly daytime now. I pulled the cover under my chin, and at the other end, as if it were something far away, my feet appeared. Both of them looking funny, and both different; both strangers to one another and as if opposed to one another, you'd say. The first one had toes that were more interesting and lively, while the second one was stumpy, wiser and all folded up in its sleep, not yet ready to get up. I spent some time looking at my thoughts jump about on my toes, from one to the other. They were like fingers on the keys of a piano, and then I got up and went downstairs to the kitchen for breakfast. And then into the addition…and then, every-where on the farm.

It was during the summer vacation, which would last for some time still. I walk, I watch…and I know that I walk and I watch. I speak, I say hello, I keep quiet and I know how to say nothing. What remains of the sun and the summer is here. It's Sunday and it's early in the morning. And I find myself thrown into another, almost normal day in the month of August, with the birds flying next to one another from our courtyard to our neighbour's just across the way. This Sunday, it's an end-of-summer morning; the foliage is still green and rustles noisily as if it wanted to warn us that a beast was hiding in the surroundings. But nothing more, and to those that don't pay attention to this sort of thing, you'd say that there was nothing there. There you have it. I don't know what else to say. I'm not capable of naming it more precisely, either. In this long French composition that is my summer homework assignment, you could say that words don't serve me well and that my dictionary is a tomb-stone at the bottom of the water. I walk, I watch, and for me, until tomorrow, it's still the summertime.

Today, the best thing I can do is to keep working on my composition, structured like a movie. At the house, they say that I'm funny. Today, the best thing that I can do is to wait, like in the film, for the monster to come up the river. But nothing else.

In the morality course in school, I've certainly tried to say that I'm being watched, but my teacher said: "Tut-tut... You read too many books. Charles, all the people around you love you..." and it didn't go any further.

There you have it. If I don't speak, I've just given the reason why. Speaking, it seems to me, wouldn't do anything anyway, and furthermore, speaking, as I've already said, is reserved for those who don't have anything to say.

During the first few days, I remember he didn't say a thing. During the first few days, he worked non-stop, and in order to get him to come to the table and eat my mother had to call him several times. He'd then sit shyly and not say anything...without looking at anyone, either. At that time, I think that if he'd wanted anything, he wouldn't have asked for it.

He would eat quickly, too, holding the edge of his plate, and the Shadows said that it was as if he were afraid there wasn't enough to eat.

After, he'd get up from the table, without excusing himself or anything, then go and sit down in a corner all alone.

That was when he was still antisocial, when he'd say nothing to the others. Although at times, he started telling me things about his past. When he came to get me at the village barbershop a few weeks after his arrival, he'd said that Ontario was warmer than here and that the land was richer there and there were fruits and golf courses everywhere. As for me, I just kept looking around and didn't believe it.

On the road, he walked – and already I'd noticed that he acted like a child – with a stick in his hand, hitting it off stones, like only little kids do: looking down with his shoulders rounded.

I think this is why we had trouble understanding what he was saying. Because of his head tucked into his shoulders, but it was also in part because of his choice of words.

For example, he kept saying Windsor. He kept saying that he had relatives in Windsor; people lived there like we live in the city, but who spoke English all the time, always *ready* is what he kept saying. And without knowing it, he had begun humiliating me. He had said: "There's not nothin' but treeless fields around these parts…" and then he stopped talking. We'd arrived at the house.

In my composition, in order to not be too direct while speaking about the monster, I didn't write:

He uses words like netteyer *(nettoyer),* caltron *(carton) and* bacul *(palonnier).*[8] *To say the word* fourchette *(fork), he says something that sounds like* couchette, *and now he shows that he's still hungry by raising his dish and saying: "Huh…" He also says, like English speakers say sometimes in French: my mine, you yours, count one, twos, threes…. He invented the verb* arvenir — *he says: "J'arviens,"*[9] *meaning, I'm coming — and sometimes, he stutters, but most often, he doesn't say anything when there are people around.*

In my composition, still about the Ornithorhynchus, I made a silly mistake because I shouldn't have written in my plan:

He isn't tall, stocky and solid on his feet; has dentures — two; one up top and one on the bottom — a gift for walking with his fly open, blowing his dirty nose on his sleeve, spying, knowing everything and making fun sometimes.

This other sentence, too:

He says words in English, words in French and other words that I don't know. He continues on his way, hits stones with his stick and blows his dirty nose on his sleeve...

In June, while reading the plan for my summer homework assignment, my teacher pointed this out: "Do you really believe that an Ornithorhynchus wears a shirt with sleeves?" I said: "I think so..."

She raised her horn-rimmed glasses.

I've already mentioned this: my teacher is part of that percentage of teachers that speak in order to say nothing. As for me, I'm becoming a specialist in historical inventions. Or an inventor of tales. You'll understand: the more we go on, the more I have difficulty saying things directly. The further I advance in my composition, the more I put on masks and the more I create detours and set up smokescreens.

After mass, he said: "I got the saddle outta the hangar."

I said: "Dad, I want to go with you."

He said: "Yer gonna like it. We're gonna get up on the bay mare.

I said: "I want to go to town today."

And he said, while raising his voice so that it would be heard clearly:

"The animal isn't well-trained an' I don't think I'm capable a grabbin' it all by myself. I'd need a *helper*. When the horse is scared, by nothin' but a guy, it can take the whole afternoon *to be runnin'* after it." And then he stopped talking. He didn't say anything else for a while, and then after said: "When we go back down, I'll put the saddle on it. Ya can get up on top…" And while saying this, he was looking at my father as if I didn't count in the end.

There was a moment, something like a moment of silence, a moment and I couldn't undo it. There was another moment that arose due to an irrational fear, a moment that I had to surrender to because I didn't know what was going to happen.

Father took advantage of it to say: "I don't know what time I'm going to be back at home. Sometimes, it takes a long time, that there business. Ya'd be better to stay here and go for a ride…without that, he won't be able to bring it back all alone. There's nothing fun for ya in town. Usually, ya like that, going for a ride?… With me you're gonna do nothing but wait." He then added: "Right… I gotta go. If ya don't want to go riding, ya'll have to go down with the others that are going to spread manure. Right!… I gotta go."

The other one, he said: "C'mon on over here right away. Put on yer boots. The grass is maybe still wet." He said: "Brin' me my umbrella, then look under the dresser in my room… There's gotta be some candies. Bring 'em to me."

When my father says: "I gotta go" this is always the last sentence that he pronounces, and this even if he hasn't said a lot before. And this even if there's still something you still have to say. Past experience tells me that when he says this, you know the debate is over. Most often, you stay there with words in your mouth, with so many words filling your mouth that they get mixed up and stuck when trying to get out.

He put on his galoshes, his jacket and asked for his wallet. Then, he got into the Ford truck.

My father even had a title in my story and it's something like "The Abandoner." I forgot. Even if I'm the one who gave him this title, as with the Shadows and the Ornithorhynchus, there's a lot. What I need is a glossary or even another dictionary about the same size, a "pocket dictionary" that I could take everywhere or, better still, something that would have my own pages in it and that I could add to my *Petit Larousse Illustré*. Because, that's the one that I like the most.

That's where I find words, pictures and maps; maps of cities, too… and machines that they take apart in it, right in front of my eyes. And photos – if I know all about the things on a film set, that's why – portraits and other information on movies. It's thick and full of marvellous things. At nighttime sometimes, I sleep with my head laid on it, for real.

I put on my boots and went into his room to get the chocolate bar that he'd left there. People can always get me to do things that I don't want to do, but I don't do it gladly …that's for sure. At the *Grande Montée*, I kept far from him. And the rest of the way, I walked at a good distance as if he were dirty and stunk. This is also partly the case.

Too much contact with animals made it so that he smelled bad. He had bad breath, and I notice this when he attempts to play with me. Most of the time, I refuse because I find he smells so bad, that his dentures are so dirty, and that his nose runs so much and everything.

It's true, though, that I often let myself get tricked and end up running right into the walls of my fishbowl. I'll admit this, but also know that I can resist, too, and get my own back. People always get me, okay, but I'm a fish that bites and you don't get me with impunity, as I have learned to say. And because I find that this is a fine word, impunity, I repeat it in my head, as if it were a song that had only one word. While walking: "impunity, impunity…"

I murmur the word when I find myself cornered by him, by his logic which shuts me up, and makes me his victim, albeit still rebellious. I chant it, too, on the way to school, when thinking about being in composition class and when I've applied myself to something and then failed at it. They didn't ask me my opinion, just like when there's an attacker, first of all, and then right away after, his witness. I believe that the witness is the most important of the two, when it comes down to it. Because he's there when I come undone; it's when he's present that I always lose. I know that we shouldn't say always, but… My father, once again, played his role as the witness and became an accomplice to the monster. And for me, this is the most important thing. Witness – sometimes it can be a synonym for Abandoner.

In composition class, I didn't write:

I know now that the enemy has a double.

Could it be that a father uses certain expressions deliber-
ately to annoy his son? "The youngest of the boys," as he's
enjoyed saying sometimes, which is an expression that embar-
rasses me because, until now, he's done all he can so that this
expression harms me. When he repeats this short phrase,
which in itself is nothing, it's like I was hearing "the smallest,"
"the silliest," the "most incapable" of them all. It's like, because
those words come from the Abandoner, that they were nastier,
crueler or had a meaning other than the one that the diction-
ary gives. I don't know anymore.

I didn't write this either, because it's too serious.

Could it be that a father is bad for his child? Could it be,
as I've come to notice, that he's an enemy spy behind my lines;
undermining my plans, revealing my strategies and only pre-
tending when saying that I can count on him? How can you
tell or know? It's a war and who do you trust when you're my
age? All I can do today is question the composition that I'm
doing. How is it that the enemy, coming back up the river, is
of my race and that the crime he's readying himself to commit
is permitted by Washington? My father, could you not have
stopped the Ornithorhynchus before he committed the
irreparable?

That Sunday, he walked slowly; sometimes if he stopped, I
did the same thing. And if the pause lasted too long, I'd step
off the dirt trail right then and there and head out on a side

path. After, he'd start off again, shouting sometimes: "Come"... and I didn't answer him. I kept my head down, slowed up and dragged my hand in the water of the reservoir. This was at the *Grande Montée*. The alcove, where we put the bulls out to pasture and where you find cherry trees.

I was wearing boots, but the dew had been there for a long time and the colour of the land was beautiful, I must say. The weather was a bit muggy, but just a bit, and if I had known these days better, I'd have said that the weather was stormy. I didn't dare, however; you don't know this being a child. Not me, at least, not yet in any case; I only had suspicions with respect to things. As for him, he was going up the hill in the dry grass with his golf umbrella on his shoulder. There were a few clouds, but no more than that. The land was dusty and you could hardly distinguish the furrows left by the Shadows who had gone to spread manure early in the morning.

The weather was stormy, so much so that the boots I put on to protect me from the dew will help protect me against the rain, which will turn the trail into a hot-watered, muddy river. And we didn't know this. We were making our way up, him about two hundred feet ahead of me; me behind, keeping this distance as we passed by the enclosed pastures. We were one behind the other, like and exactly like, when he had newly arrived at our place and was the one who would come get me at the barbershop in the village.

I'd spent all afternoon waiting to get my hair cut and then after, to be picked up. Out of the bay window that gives onto the main street, he was the one I saw coming. I remember he entered with his boots on, all sweaty, because it was summer, and that he said to the barber, because he never spoke directly to me:

"His mother was worried an' then ask'd that I get him..." and I also remember that I'd been happy. Because at the time, he was still "the good innocent one who knew how to do everything," as Dad had said, which was what we were all thinking. And this, so much so, as he knew how to be helpful and because he put so much heart into his work.

It hadn't been long since he'd been living with us and he was generous. I remember that for me, he always had candies and that he called them indifferently "candies," whether they were sweets, Popeye cigarettes or chocolates. He said "candies" and the others, my brothers and sisters, the ones that were going to be called the Shadows, they laughed. This lasted some time. After, when they got used to it, they made as if they didn't hear him. As I've already said: I'm the only one who seems surprised by the way he talks.

He was the one who had come to get me in the village and we'd left one after the other because we were uncomfortable talking; hands in our pockets. And me, I dragged my feet just like him; one after the other, too, because the cars go fast, because they're in a rush on the gravel road. It was summer. The real one, the hot one, with an afternoon sun that was beating down on my freshly shaven neck. We were making our way up. I don't know anymore if it was because of the sun or because of the steepness of the path, but the cologne that the barber put on me was getting to me… Anymore, and I wouldn't have been able to hear the buzz of the flies and wasps that were flying around me. On our way up, from one parcel of land to another, one farm to another, meeting a tractor sometimes with someone we knew in it or a car that was going fast with a driver that we didn't know. We were passing by the enclosed pastures and leaving the village behind us with the church's reflection in the river.

Upon arriving at the first gate to our land, he had said: "Look, there's a car that was park'd there last night. Do ya know what they stopp'd there for, right there, ya know in the open field?"…but I hadn't understood. I've already said: it was a few years ago. He was still new at our place and he was still alright with me, even when there wasn't anyone watching us.

That there Sunday, at first there was the *Grande Montée*, the one which is just behind our house, and then, the farm buildings. It's perhaps the most abrupt one in all my father's land and which, like an initiation, once you've gone through it, provides you with a spectacular view of the land that's sometimes hilly, sometimes flat and all cut up by the rivers, the fields, the ravines and the trees.

In winter, we use our toboggans and slide down the *Grande Montée*.

After, there was the *Peupliers Cassés*, which is a nice flat part that, in time, we learned to exploit. There, he stopped, thinking for a moment that I was going to catch up with him, but I stopped, too.

He waited a few minutes, I don't know how long, turned around and then continued on. In the field, like a tree. I walked on. He didn't say anything and sometimes turned his head, maybe just to check if I was still behind. Maybe, and that's what I thought, just to show me that he was thinking about me. We kept going up.

Once at *Timothy-en-bas* – a funny piece of land made up of two parts in which one makes up a plateau in terms of the other – I went by the spring and into the barn. This is where we store the tools and equipment during winter and a little bit of hay when we notice that there's no more room in the stable and that we have to separate the stocks of food.

It was a building with walls made of grey planks, for the most part, that were sort of wet-like. Its roof had been sealed and solid in its day, but was now full of holes because of missing tiles, ripped off by the wind. Once there, I went around him, at least ten feet from him perhaps, without turning my head. It was terribly quiet all around.

After the barn, there's *Tim-en-haut*, which is a strip of land much longer than it is wide. It's situated between a coulee stretching out towards the summer pastures and the neighbours' fields and closed off by a fence. Suddenly, a cooler wind, you'd say, started to blow and you could see its direction in the grass. The word that came to mind was "gust,"[10] but I knew that this wasn't the correct word for that particular type of wind. I was disappointed.

Would I ever like to be in the know in terms of the weather and the seasons. Is it going to rain? Is it going to be nice out? Will the mounds of oats be dry, too? Those are the questions that I'd like answers to. This, and to know all the words having to do with the land and their precise meaning.

Like a groundhog, I'd also like to know if the spring will go by quickly or not, and like the wasps, be able to foresee the amount of snow for an entire winter. I'm interested in this type of thing.

I'd gotten a little farther than the barn when I heard something that sounded like a burp. He was following me:

He was walking at some fifty feet from me and tried to catch me... I ran.

After, it's *Chez Rose*, which is also a peculiar piece of land because it's all lacey. It has ravines all along it and over-flows like a chocolate stain in the sun. It's a bubble seeking to burst forth, which folds back on itself, and that some-times manages to break through and there's a leak. *Chez Rose*, that's the way it is. It's a vast chocolate stain – a par-cel trying to get away in the grass. From everywhere, whether it be towards the forest or between the ravines, there are points sticking out that stretch like tongues getting pointier, little by little.

That's *Chez Rose* and it's also the end of the land up top. After that, to stay on our land, you'd need to make a fork in the road, go left and go back from where we started in order to get back into the summer pastures.

I took the path that goes towards *Clos-à-Julie* and he followed me, silently, while respecting the distance I'd established and looking around if I turned my head to see him. He was walking with his back arched, hanging onto the saddle perched on his shoulder, and was taking fast, little steps, and too many of them, as if in a rush to get it over with. He was looking up into the sky while making faces, as if he'd wanted to show me there would be rain and the land would become muddy and that we didn't have any time to waste, either. He stayed like that the whole way along. Walking with his red and white umbrella, and waiting for the storm.

Under a tree, the little horse waited. This was no doubt due to habit, as the afternoon air, which had become cooler, didn't warrant the wait. We were going to put the halter around it.

He said: "Can ya keep yerself still while I put the saddle on ya?"

He said: "Yer quite plump. She's good here. There was tons of hay. Do ya wanna get up? Don't get goin' away there, *mon voleur...*"

He walked around the mare as if he were interested in her and kept talking either to me or the horse, it didn't matter. He said: "My li'l *Nouère*...yer time's up. We're gonna look after ya."[11]

He said: "Ya ain't that skittish. I won't hurt ya."

He put the bridal over the halter, girthed the beast and was doing all sorts of manoeuvres just like you do when rigging up a boat. The horse was calm, more than I'd first imagined it to be. It let him do his thing without rearing up and accepted its loss of freedom, as if it had been waiting for just that. Foxes. Foxes.

He said: "Yer quite plump, my love."

He said: "Don't get goin'... I ain't gonna hurt ya. Let go a bit. It won't be long."

He said: "Give me a paw, my love. There...that's it...again a paw..." and he kept touching the animal all over, letting his hand slide on its back, then towards the rump, then returned to it for no reason in order to pat the mare on the forehead. Like he wanted to reassure it, and then, he kept on doing it.

I was standing up, about ten feet from him. I knew that he was talking to the animal, but I didn't understand what he was saying. Maybe I wasn't really listening, hearing? There was the sound of the wind in the dry leaves and it was making a distracting rustle. As for him, I could hear him complaining, and it was like a chant. I couldn't make out the words. I didn't know anymore if they were words.

There's certainly always a rhythm that is produced when a hand goes back and forth and that becomes softer with each passing. But, I can say that it wasn't quite like that, then.

Him, with his fingers that are usually numb, he managed to create some sort of harmony between man and beast. Until then, this ability was entirely unsuspected on my behalf and was ignored by the others, too, I think.

When a body moves, you can always feel a little dance or a beat in the air, but the relationship between the monster and the beast wasn't of that order.

In my composition, I didn't say that, in a certain way, the monster must have known the power of words. I couldn't say that either and that because he was a beast, he was attracted to animals' bodies. I had to content myself with writing words that are spoken.

And the more things move along, the more I realize that in my composition I didn't write what was important.

The mare was moving more and as I was standing just next to it, I could hear them breathing, her and him, when all of a sudden and in a loud voice, he said: "It's ready, ya can climb up." I no longer knew whether I was supposed to accept this, like the horse earlier, or flee by running away as the horse hadn't done.

Because the stirrup was high, he gave me a hand up. In the saddle, I felt at ease. He said: "Do ya want me to hold the halter at first?" I said no. I said: "Let me do it..." and, like in the movies, I gave a little kick of my heels while, and precisely while, I was pulling back on the reins. The horse turned around on the spot and we started off. A fine and light rain started to fall.

When did it begin? Was it the first day of baling hay when, because of a broken piece of the scythe-bailer,[12] we had to go together to find another part at our neighbour's place?... Or that morning, when sowing the seeds in the garden? That morning when he said that the radishes would become as big as balls and the broad beans would look like my privates, and that when adolescence came about, I'd be dirty and smell bad like potatoes rotting away in the furrows since last year? I don't know anymore.

How was I to know and be precise with life, when you can't be, even when writing a composition? The day of the scythe-bailer and the race to the neighbour's place doesn't mean a thing. He was definitely talking non-stop about "his photas" and the apartment that he'd have...but it seems to me that my uneasiness doesn't date back to that time. And when we were sowing the garden, I was already afraid of him and knew already that I shouldn't trust him.

To this question "When did it all begin?" I should answer that it all dates back to before the summer, near Easter or even further back, near Christmas...to the time when I surprised him drinking in the bed of the old Ford, for example.

I remember that after lunch, my father sent me to get something from the stable when I noticed prints in the snow near the truck. I knew that it was him and I opened the door. I've already said that he was the only big person who acted like a kid. That day, he'd hidden himself in the box with some alcohol. After, he lay down flat out on the wooden truck bed and kept drinking with his tuque and mittens on.

He said: "Hey, thingamajig..." And when he says "Hey, thingamajig," I don't answer right away and wait for the rest. Even if it takes a while sometimes. Even if he looks at me with his eyes turned up.

He said: "Don't be goin' tellin' nobody nothin'. It's nothin' but a bottle of liquor. Do ya want any?" and I hadn't moved or said anything. He kept on talking while letting the alcohol flow down his frozen chin.

He said: "Who is it that's the cleanest between a man an' a woman?" I wanted to say a woman, but he didn't give me the time to respond and then added: "A woman's all bloody." I didn't say anything. He had a few more swigs and wanted to break a bit of ice with his boot and said: "Yer heartless, you. Come sits here in the bed. It's Chrissmis! Here...take some, a mouthful. It's good. Yer freezin' there, but ya won't be after. I bought it myself..." and, as I wasn't saying anything back, he continued on to another subject in order to get me.

I swear he's cunning. I've already said that his tactic is to lay it on thick. Another one of his favourite strategies is to jump from one subject to another when you're being quiet. He hopes that in this way he'll breach your silence and impose himself. That's the way things go.

He was stretched out on the frozen piece of plywood on a cold winter's and I tried to forget this.

Does my nightmare date back to this moment? This is a question I can't answer. My composition shows the slow procession of the Ornithorhynchus on the river; but when did it all really start? Is it the day that my father said that I was supposed to help him with his chores, or before when he was new at our place and he let me see the fabulous objects that he had in his bags? I can't answer this because, for the moment, I don't have an answer to give. And I ask questions because in order to understand, I owe it to myself to go back there. Sometimes, it seems to me that the monster is so crafty.

He even found a technique. Or a means. Just to make sure he bugs me…and to make himself happy. He invented a word, too, a new one, derived from the verb *sentir* – meaning to sense, smell and feel. I've already said that he takes shortcuts with words, that one there. He says:

"Let me scents ya…" and my story this morning becomes truly intolerable because he wants me to put my hands in my underwear and show them to him after. He says:

"Let me scents ya a bit…" and then he added: "It's not a big deal; I won't touch," as if he imagined that touching was the only thing that counted. It was like he was thinking that he could do anything if he doesn't touch or if he isn't touched. He's a big mongoloid and his words are monstrous. His hands are dirty and his eyes are ugly. What's more, he's always behind my back, like I said. I repeat: he speaks poorly and smells bad. I think that there aren't enough subtleties in my dictionary to describe this stinky monster that won't let me be.

Also, in my composition, he didn't say: "*Come... After it'll be too late. Come... Don't be goin' tellin' nobody nothin'. Come...let me scents ya...*"

In my composition, he didn't say: "*A mare, it's like a woman... Look. It's soft an' clean. Ya'd say that it has toilet paper...has candies...*"

He couldn't say either: "*Come... Don't be goin' tellin' nobody nothin'*" and in my composition he didn't add: "*...but I'm bad off here. This ain't my place here in the treeless fields...then sometimes, I wanna drown myself...*"

Yet, he threw his head back, making gurgling sounds with the rainwater, for real, and then after, the slobber ran down his chin. He was making noise, a ruckus, with his arms and his feet...and it was time for his act. He kept saying: "I wanna drown myself." No more seriously though than if "drown" had been something else, as he was always taking liberties with words.

In my composition, I watched him do it without saying a thing. He was gurgling but wasn't saying "scents ya" and wasn't saying "drown."

We say "in the heart of the summer" and the summers at
our place are hot and dry and the dirt trails become
crevassed sometimes. In autumn, because of the rain on
the clay, it becomes like, and exactly like, a muddy water-
shed that runs between the grass. So, you never know
when you'll be able to use the road. Because a horse in
the mud is a horse in the snow. It worries you and it
slides. And in the stacks of hay, the enemy could hide
standing up.

Moreover, my father's land is a capharnaum[13] of sorts, if
you see what I mean, and want to know. And because of all
its nooks and crannies, you never really know for sure which
way will be the shortest, or which way will be the most practical for the Ford truck or the tractor. On certain days of the
year, it really is the Abandoner's country. There's a sort of
inherent mystery to the land itself, this land that the family has owned for four generations and that it roams all over
in all directions, and every day. It makes up a patchwork of
ill-assorted meadows and enclosed bits. It's a corner of the
country where you've got to expect anything and everything.

When I went by "the barn at *Timothy*" thinking that I
was far in front of him, I was surprised to find him there,
leaning up against the wall which faces downward, and so
well hidden that I stumbled upon him all of sudden. I just
came across him like that, and when he grabbed the halter
solidly and held the horse back, I couldn't find anything else
to say but:

"How did you manage to get here? How did you manage to get here?"

The Abandoner's country… Sometimes, I happen to have doubts about all this. What I mean is that I happen to doubt that all this really exists. Like this valley, with its land, rising on each side of a road that snakes its way along like a river in the bottom of a ravine. Lands and farms… One of the richest is the Abandoner's, with its fine house and buildings. With its monster, its Shadows and its Cake Eater. I happen to think that all this exists only in my head. On my body, there's no trace whatsoever. And in my composition, around the words, an emptiness has set in.

As if I was seeing nothing at all.

As if I was hearing nothing at all.

Or as if, by keeping quiet all the time, a hole has been hollowed out.

He wants me to hold his hand. I say no. He says:

"Just a li'l…" He says:

"Not for a long time." He says:

"Again…it's not a big deal." And I don't say anything back. I lower my head and I hide my hands.

Sometimes when he's tired and we have to get to the farm from the top of the field, he asks:

"Gimme yer hand, will ya?" and me, I say no. I run, I take off on the side paths and abandon the trail then and there. I've got to.

Yet sure enough, he finds a technique. Or a means. In order to bug me, that's for sure, and to make himself happy, too. He invented a word once again and it's a word that comes from the verb *gratter*, meaning to scratch or itch. I've already said that when he's with me, he takes liberties with words. He dares – covering his mouth with his hand because it embarrasses him a little – he dares say to me: "Come gratch me," and makes a gesture with his hand that leaves no doubt with respect to where this verb comes from; a verb not present in my *Petit Larousse*.

He says: "Come gratch me," and establishes a whole program of activities that provided the supposed sensation.

He says: "When ya ride a bike, it gratches." He says: "Saddlin' up, too, is for gratchin'…an' wearin' underwear that's too tight…it's all the same thin'…" and I notice that he covers his mouth with his hand when he says this.

He laughs, acts like an idiot, fools around but, rest assured, he's not entirely unaware of what he's doing. That's what he does, sure enough. I know that he wouldn't dare say it if anybody else were there. In front of the others, he says yes or *carrect*. He says "kay" or "right away"; he crawls, he says: "Yes, right away" and then tries to blend in, in order to better sneak about, that's for sure. And maybe, too, like with simple gestures, in order to establish his power over me.

In my composition, I wrote:

"The more we move along, the more I realize that the Ornithorhynchus becomes visible when swimming in the river. His teeth, his whole muzzle…and his colour, too, make it so that it's now impossible to mix up the monster with a chunk of wood."

I'm the wanderer.

After, I added:

A monster is on the lookout, spies, gurgles and then jumps on his prey when the time comes. But, I didn't go any further.

The horse, since it was a horse that was going to its death, let itself be mastered right away and even when I told it to turn around with my heels and start running with the movement of my wrist…regardless of the direction. The horse was done, and my attempts remained fruitless.

He said: "It won't last long. Come down from there" …and the nature of the light, almost right away, began to change.

He added: "We're gonna put the mare in the shelter."

I didn't want to get down, but a horse is not a fence handrail. He was holding it by the bridle, made it go around the mounds of oats and then brought it into the barn. And I felt ridiculous for letting myself get fooled so easily.

He said: "Look…it's gettin' wet right now. It's dangerous in the hills when it's muddy. The *cheval*[14] can slide on ya, then crush yer leg. Not long ago, it happened to a guy'n the village. Hadda cut his leg off. It's true what I'm tellin' ya there. Just ask yer father an' see…" I just want to point out that he has a whole set of abracadabra stories to make you shiver, as if his goal or his pleasure in life was to scare others. And, it was him; he was the one who told me to watch my back. Sometimes with me, he manages to succeed and sometimes he runs into a wall. I've learned in time that his success has coincided most often with the attention that I give him or when I listen to him. More and more, I force myself to not even hear what he says…and even, if for the most part, they're only grunts, slobberings and burps.

When he spits, and he happens to do this often, I try not to look at the green and slimy gob of spit spread all over the dry clay or in the wet grass in the morning. I also try to forget that he goes to the bathroom outside, and that just before, he gets rhubarb leaves to use. I try to forget all this;

that he's always hot, with pools of sweat everywhere, that his dentures are not washed and that his eyes are turned up. That's the Ornithorhynchus; the monster that knows how to sneak about and dig things up.

He said: "Come down from the mare."

He said: "You'd say that ya wanna do her all by yerself."

But I didn't get down. I have to say that I wanted to continue on my way, and that I didn't know where to go anymore.

I said: "It isn't raining anymore now. I'm sure that there hasn't been enough time for the land to get soaked through. We should go right away. If the rain starts up again, the trails will be muddy later on, for sure." But he didn't answer me.

Slowly, like in a ceremonial ritual, he went around the mare that I was sitting on and stopped behind, straight in a line with me and the beast.

I said: "Well, I'm going down right away. For me, it's not getting wet that fast...it'll be worse soon, for sure..." And as I was turning around with the horse, he was still standing behind blocking the door and said: "Wait, it shouldn't be long."

I said: "You never know how long it's going to last."

He said: "At the house, they won't be happy if ya go down all by yer lonesome in a rainstorm. Yer too young to go horse ridin' when it gets wet. Yer father won't find it *carrect*. Wait a li'l bit, still. It's gonna pass."

I said: "Shove over, I'm going down all the same..." and that's when he said: "If ya continue to do what ya want, yer gonna make the mare lose its foal. Yer always harming us. Yer father said so…'We don't want any trouble here.'"

He always has witnesses in his corner and I've noticed that it works with me. He imprisons me. A spider, a net… Often, it's like a drowning, too. Or better still, getting bogged down in the mud and water. Or better yet, it's a suction that attracts you and prevents you from walking and working and, in the end, brings you down.

How much time do I still have to wait? In my composition, in order to speak about childhood and boats, I said: *"The short reach of my long arms prevents me from grasping the world…"* but nothing more.

In my composition, I always have to dress and distort people and cover up the facts. Without this, there could be grave consequences.

He continues to invent words – scents, gratch – but he doesn't stop there. He invents gestures, too. Sometimes, for nothing and without us even talking, he shows me the end of his finger and laughs. After, he'll move on to something else, it depends. But the important thing is that he's trying to give me a sign and let me know what he's interested in.

In my composition, I wrote:

The Ornithorhynchus makes noise with his paws on the river. The wanderer turns his head and he knows that he's there.

But I didn't write:

Could it be that one of the combat tactics is to make others feel, sense, or smell his presence? Might it be that in war, that the only words worth anything are to hide, to be on the lookout, to spy?

He's watching me. And he wants me to know he's watching me. Behind a door, or when we're alone near the stable. If he doesn't have the time for storytelling, he shows me his finger. Like that sergeant with the colonel in the film, he doesn't want me to forget he's there.

It's incredible just how loud the noise is from raindrops falling on a rusty tin roof.

He was standing in front of the door, and even if he'd let go of the mare, the rain, which had started again, dissuaded me from leaving. Because of the rainstorm the weather was cooler, and again, because of the rainstorm, a half-light had settled in. There, right between the ploughing equipment that wouldn't get moved until next summer. It was there, too, on the remaining bit of hay that was shrivelling up in the humidity of an autumn that hadn't yet happened.

Him, he was going counter-clockwise and me, I was still up on the horse's back, observing him from the corner of my eye. I saw him line himself up with it and come back from behind; I also saw him make a straight line with me and the mare. I heard him laugh and breathe deeply. I waited for him to speak and he said:

"Ya dunno the difference between a mare and a stallion, do ya?"

If you want to know if someone is going to start acting up, I'm a specialist. He always laughs a bit just before.

He was behind me and his voice was carrying as if he were talking right in my ear. It was still a whisper, but loud. On the T.V., this would have corresponded to raising the volume without changing the channel. For him, this detail didn't matter and he said: "Ya dunno, do ya? Ya must be too young to know these types a things." Then, he added: "Stallions and mares, together, they do what li'l boys an' girls do when they're in the playground."

Between my teeth, I whistled something like: "I could have sworn" because I know the rules of the game: it's always him answering the question that he's just asked.

As soon as we're alone, and this is the reason that I avoid him, he starts talking about dirty things and if he doesn't do it right away, you can be certain that he's going to talk around it. Ah, as far as that's concerned… he's going to talk around it…

It always begins with a question which seems completely harmless, something like: "Ya dunno the difference, do ya…" or something like: "Do ya know when she was young…" or even something that's more familiar and that begins by: "Don't be goin' tellin' nobody nothin'…" And he'd ramble on about something that often made hardly any sense and which often concerns people that I don't know, but that deals with smut, no doubt about that. It's always like this with him.

Most of the time, I take off. Sometimes, when like today, it's impossible, I don't listen to him. Sometimes, I even tell him – and this is a threat that he quickly makes work of neutralizing – that I'm going to tell on him and that he doesn't have the right to say things like that to a child, and that he can even go to prison like we heard on the radio about the kids in Mexico.

When I say this, he groans and says I was the one who started it, and adds that he's the one who's going to tell on me, by saying: "I'm gonna say that ya gotta phota, with a li'l girl on it who's goin' pee and all…"

His technique is to lay it on thick; so much so that in the end I don't know how to defend myself against him. And for him to stop, even just a little bit, I'd beg him on my hands and knees. His tactic is to submerge me in it. He throws lots of things at me that make no sense, and I find myself the prisoner of a logic that tries to untangle it all. As a result, he laughs with a voice that isn't one anymore, especially when he's excited and gets all muddled. He stutters, especially when he's been the strongest, you'd say. And so then again, he laughs, and his laugh is frankly nasty.

And I'm always surprised to see how, although he's nothing more than a mongoloid in front of others, he develops this confidence of sorts with me. He uses his authority when he's all alone with me, but it's always linked to the others. I think that if I were really alone with him, he wouldn't have all this power, because it always has to do with the others. By means of suggestion is perhaps how he gets his way. And I'm a bit stunned to find someone manipulating me when I'm alone and while using other people. I'm sure that if I were to try to explain this in my next composition, I wouldn't get ten out of ten in logic. It's too difficult a subject. At this stage, I can only express my uneasiness or my doubt or my fear. No dictionary can come to my rescue. Not even my *Petit Illustré* where you can of course find the word "satyr," but that is associated with "divinity"… And this without photos or anything.

He said: "A mare is just like a woman. Did ya know that, you there?"

He also said: "It's round an' clean…an' it likes that, being petted. You, yer too young to understand these kinds'a things. How old are ya, huh?"

He stayed behind my back, talking to himself all alone, wiggling, and me, I kept trying not to listen to him and didn't answer him.

He said: "Get down an' then come an' see from behind… Yer gonna see how a woman an' a mare are the same. Come see. Ya've already seen pictures of women? Look at a mare an' the way it's made…an' it's always clean. Ya'd say that it has toilet paper. It's soft…"

The horse wiggled, and I turned around only to see him pulling on its tail from behind…[15]

It was raining harder and harder and because I was trying not to listen to him, he wouldn't stop talking and making gestures which, without a doubt, were obscene. Suddenly, I felt tired. He stopped talking, and all of a sudden I knew what he was doing. He kept saying: "Look…I can put my fingers in…" and me, I wouldn't turn my head to see.

He kept on, saying: "Look. I'm puttin' my thumb in…the big finger on the edge…" but I wouldn't turn my head to look.

I knew he did this type of thing sometimes, especially in the summer. I still remember that he kept telling me that the other farmers around — and he would give their names — would do the same thing sometimes. He kept saying that it's good, naming a whole bunch of respectable men who, according to him, would play this game with cows because, and he was the one who said this, "sometimes it's better than a woman."

Sometimes the mare would make an abrupt movement and sometimes she would stay still and stiff, undergoing what I supposed was a humiliation.

In my composition, I didn't write:

It's strange. It's the monster, himself, telling me to watch my back. He says that others do dirty things, that they wouldn't hesitate to slit my throat, and has once again no problem telling me their names. He says: so and so, and so and so...

It's funny. It's been quite a while now, but I'm still stunned to see that the monster prefers to put me on my guard.

I got down from the horse and then, without speaking and without looking back, I moved towards the door while trying not to listen, either. It was pouring rain. Without a doubt, the rain would continue for a long time and we'd have to go down on foot, abandoning an already dead horse in the barn. A whole morning wasted...with rain all around and pouring down on the roof of a rotten barn in a field at the beginning of autumn. Without us really being able to do anything about it.

Seeing the speed at which he caught up with me, I noticed that what I had understood at first had not really happened or, better still, that he had only made the first moves.

All I can say about this is that I was surprised to see him so quick and to find him instantly at the barn door and a little bit behind my back, making as if he were interested in the rain, as if he had to present the weather on the television.

He was talking about the miry paths and saying:

"Yers isn't much bigger than that..." and added "that we couldn't get back to the house in time to eat." He kept saying while looking at the water fall, "gurgle, gurgle," and then: "Do ya want some *candies*?..." then: "If I could only drown myself" while sticking out his tongue and rolling his eyes...and saying, too: "There ain't no summer hereabouts."

It was very muddled and I must say I felt lost faced with this bombardment of words that weren't linked to one other.

His tactic is to lay it on thick. One of his fighting strategies is to submerge you in words in order to create a breach and get in.

He said: "Yer so young, yer so li'l..." He added: "Yer handsome for a boy. It's rare to see that, such regular features. Ya got a pushed-up nose an' it suits you, I find. In a year or two, it's gonna change, yer nose." I said: "Why?" and as soon as I fired off the question, I regretted it. It wasn't the thing to do. I make an effort not to talk to him since I know full well that he's just waiting for a chance like this one to start up again and bring up what interests him the most. And, this, I don't get wrong.

For my "why" fired off a little earlier, I was entitled to all kinds of precise explanations on what the ungrateful years are – this was his own expression – and what this time of life brought about in terms of bodily transformations. He didn't hold back any details, you can believe me...and the problems that are related to this period. He enumerated them for me in a direct and clear fashion. Methodically. I've already said that beneath his innocent exterior he knows how to make connections when it interests him. At these moments, he's a biologist coupled with a psychologist. Heavens!... To listen to him, men go through hell during adolescence.

After, I looked at the rain and noticed "it wouldn't be much longer now..." and he said, while adopting a detached tone of voice: "Show me yers. I'm gonna tell ya what's gonna happen in two years. It's easy to explain when ya see it." He said:

"Show, let's see...there's supposed to be like a li'l piece a skin. How old are ya?" he ended up saying. And this was one of the questions that he'd ask non-stop, as if my age was so important or as if something sacred depended on it.

He once again said: "Show it to me... It's not to hurt ya that I'm askin'. Sometimes, it has like a li'l piece a skin an' if it isn't off, it can end up bein' dangerous." And he continued to talk, all by himself for the most part...being used to it, as he'd developed the habit of long monologues that nothing could change due to his contact with animals.

Him, the monster: all alone and knowledgeable.

It's when he said: "If ya don't have it look'd after right away, maybe ya'll never be a man" that he sowed the seeds of doubt, breaking down the resistance I'd built up to defend myself against his words, creating a breach that his beady eyes quickly sought out. He followed up, saying:

"There are certainly some guys that can't marry today because they didn't have it look'd after when they was young. Gotta be careful. It's like a li'l piece a skin... Show me, just to see. I'm gonna tell ya if it's normal or if ya need an operation. Gotta go to the doctor, but it seems it don't even hurt. In the end, ain't nothing but a li'l bit a skin." He kept saying: "Don't be goin' tellin' nobody nothin'." He kept saying: "So and so, and so and so..." and there he kept giving me names that didn't mean a thing for the most part, but which, according to him, were men who had to go one day or another to the doctor because of this.

He said: "There's a name for that there thingamajig, but I don't remember it."

He said: "The Jews do it."

He also said: "Seems like for them there, it was a sign of being rich. Hitler didn't have it when he was young an' so that's why that he was jealous of the Jews. Do ya know who Hitler is? Ya know Hitler?..." and on this, he went into stories that were more and more macabre, but that he swore to me were real facts and true. I've already said it: because of his innocent appearance we were always surprised to learn how much he was able to retain certain things. He might not have gone to school, but he knew how to listen to others, you can be sure of that.

As usual, he concluded what he was saying by: "Ya can ask yer father if ya don't believe me... Ya ask'im what Hitler did to them Jews, just to see... Ya never believe me. I told ya that it'd stay wet for a long time."

And then, he stopped talking about Hitler.

Now, he was behind me, like he had been behind the horse earlier. I could hear him breathing and felt that he was near, as he often happens to be behind my back. As it often happens, too, he wasn't speaking, but was moving and making noise like the animals when they want something, hay for example, or water.

His accomplice the rain was weaving nets where the clouds were moving about as if agitated, flying high sometimes and then sliding down even with the earth, which had become muddy. And this, because it had been raining hard for some time. And because of a missing tile, you could see the water coming down through a hole in the roofing, making a waterfall. Here, even inside. Here, even where we thought we were protected.

I've already said that he mostly didn't say anything. But when he opened his mouth, it was to try to worry me, tell me that because of a growth — he still hadn't found the name for it and, me, I didn't say it — I might not ever be able to marry and become a man.

He said: "Show me just a li'l…just to see… I'm gonna tell ya right away if it's *carrect* or not." During this time I didn't say anything and tried not to listen to him, but he kept insisting: "Don't be afraid…"

He was stuttering: "I won't even touch, if ya don't want. I swear that I won't touch… Ya got nothin' to do but take it out a li'l an' I'm gonna tell ya right away. It's not a big deal when ya don't touch."

He didn't want to stop and I said: "Stop talking to me about that."

I said again: "You could go to prison if anyone knew. You don't have the right to say things like that to a child. I'm not sure that Father would pay to get you out... It must cost an awful lot to get someone out of prison who does things like this to kids. You'd be in prison for maybe a year or maybe more. I'm sure nobody would go see you. Then, the ones that are disgusting with kids, they're looked down on by other prisoners. You know that. They get beaten; you're aware of that. They talk about it on the radio. Most of the time you find them dead on the cement, in a corner...with rats around them, licking up the blood pouring out of them. Maybe that would be fun for you, as you never take a vacation?..." He laughed, moved his feet, made noise and didn't want to let this affect him.

What I remember is that I know how to be nasty with him.

And sometimes, I'm like the Ornithorhynchus and I use his technique, which is to lay it on thick without counting. Most often, sentences like that have the effect of frightening him a little: at other times, you'd say that he doesn't believe me and that he has answers ready to throw back at me, in any case.

He lowered his head, kept laughing his dumb little laugh, which was a little dirty, too. And that's when you could see his badly washed dentures, uncovered by his upper lip. He kept ferociously counter-attacking too, not hesitating to lie and use others as his witnesses. I've already said that when he does this, I remain completely powerless.

He said: "If ya don't let me look, I'm gonna tell everybody."

I said: "Which everybody?"

He responded: "So and so, and then so and so…"

He said: "I'm gonna tell everybody yer not normal an' that ya won't be able to get married."

I said: "That's not true."

He said: "So, let's see then… Ya don't wanna, huh. Yer afraid, huh, huh?" because that's what he did when he didn't have any words left. I have to say that his vocabulary wasn't exactly extensive. I also have to say that he's a beast and that sometimes he started saying "huh, huh" and that this could mean that he was happy or angry. It depends. He kept stuttering and added: "Yer gonna get yerself laughed at, at school when the others are gonna find out about it."

He also said: "I'm gonna tell li'l Louis about it. Him, he's not embarrassed. He can then talk to yer schoolteacher about it, too"…and he began saying "huh, huh"…which was a sort of a laugh, I think. And if I tried to say that I was going to tell on him, he wouldn't even listen anymore, that's for sure.

Him, he was going to tell on me.

Him, he'd tell the others…

Who? My father, my mother, my brothers and sisters…my friends at school and then the teacher and this one and that one…how bad I was.

"Yer a li'l devil…" he kept saying. "A li'l devil." That was his word.[16]

I heard our tractor and I shouted. The rain was drumming on the roof and there was the wind in the trees. And I shouted, as it seemed I should do.

Because they were coming back from spreading the manure and especially because they didn't want to get stuck in a drenched, dirt road, they carried on by. Very quickly.

The tractor added to the noise of the water on the roof…and they were now far away. I've already said it: the Shadows are of no help to me. In my composition I could have not included them.

Where was I again?

When did it all begin? Eight, nine or ten months ago…or just a few days ago or a few hours as I sometimes happen to think. Maybe the alcohol incident in the winter has nothing to do with it, no more than the difference in cleanliness between men and women concerns me. How can you tell or know? And how do you deal with issues which to this day, as far as I know, shouldn't have anything to do with me. At school, at home, they're quick to use the tut-tut…and I get nowhere.

One thing is for sure. When it comes to these things, my dictionary is useless to me. Maybe I should look elsewhere, but first I'd have to have leads and I don't have any. The Abandoner has no books, and if the Shadows read, it's newspapers, magazines, or even things that are so dumb it leads me to believe, sometimes, that I'm the most mature in this family. Me…the one that they call the Cake Eater. And the one they find funny and odd when I ask questions.

Can we hold the weather outside – let's say the rain – responsible for what happens to us or, on the contrary, do we have to believe that we should have been saved by it? I don't know the answer to this either. What's for sure is that a sign can be deceiving, as was the case with my rubber boots, and points of reference aren't often worth much.

I look and I watch, and I know that I'm looking and watching. I ask questions and I read. I compose… But I know that it does nothing because I'm the only one interested in it. In fact, I've become like the monster when he does his soliloquy with the animals. I almost don't laugh anymore, and if I speak, it's less and less...because my real fear is to start using words like *bacul* or like *caltron*...and my real fear is to forget my composition one day and to begin looking or acting like the monster, the Abandoner or the Shadows...like them.

I don't know if it's because of the rainstorm that grew stronger and that turned the spring into a muddy stream. I don't know if it's because of the dark, which also – was it already nighttime? – grew denser and changed quickly. When I turned around, I felt in the presence of a beast and it was too late at that moment. There was a struggle, very little, and there was a time when I had straw in my mouth. I shouted out, but it didn't prevent him from doing something that he'd never done before. He was on my back. I know that the little horse was watching us, because it was my witness. I saw her eyes shining in what had become the darkness of a day without sunlight when she didn't move, no doubt believing herself avenged for a humiliation that she had been subject to. That's the way it was. Just the way that I'm describing it. Like that. And I realize once again that there were two.

It hurt at the moment, and then after, nothing else. I had the impression that someone had gone looking for something in my body. But nothing more. That's the way it was.

September came about like the big lash of a whip that somebody very nasty would give. And it was as if, and exactly as if, we hadn't been prepared for it.

That morning at school, it hurt when I walked. Less than yesterday, okay. But when I had to run during recess, and once again when I had to bend over to tie up my laces, I felt a pain that wasn't that strong. Okay, but it was still a real wound. I think that it was swollen, and if it's not healed by the medical check-up date at the beginning of the year, I think I'll have to speak to a doctor about it. I hope I won't have to. That requires explanations and I prefer not to. I know it would be necessary for my health, but I prefer not to, that's all. And I don't care about my health right now.

With the beginning of the new year, our teacher asked us to read excerpts from our compositions. The others burst out laughing when my tongue got caught on my front palate and something came out that sounded like a burp. And yet, at first, it was nothing. But in my head, there were the words he'd said: "lookin' forward to goin' back to school..." and I couldn't stop thinking about it. It was raining, too. "Goin' back to school" like "It's the end, he said..." about the woman living by the edge of the river. These were words that were not mine.

While getting into the school bus, because of something leaking – I had the impression something was leaking in my underwear – I had to sit down alone because I thought that it would smell. I was especially afraid of this, however, Marc and my friend Louis Levasseur didn't notice a thing.

In my composition, I wrote:

My project fell through because it had to fall through.

I also wrote:

For his grandeur only and so that the tragedy remained as it should up until the end, the word that I was looking for must have been fatum.

But my teacher, who is new and doesn't know yet that I'm a specialist in historic inventions, said these sentences weren't mine. Hold on tight: it's a new teacher who corrects the work done during the summer and who gave me a bad grade while my neighbour on the left – yes, we have girls in our class – got an A. She began her composition with: "Oh! The pretty beautiful summer that we've had…" I swear I'm not inventing anything. Even if that's all that I could manage to read over her shoulder. Her subject was, of course, the summer holidays. This is what everyone always talks about in September. And I'd bet that for next year's composition, if we continue to have revolutionary teachers, it'll be the same thing once again. It was raining. And I wondered if despite all this rain, the mounds of oats could be saved.

I took up my assignment again, making it longer. I thought this way I could rid myself of the issue. By following the entire structure of the movie, I wrote:

He said to me: "Come… I've got somethin' to tell ya. Come… Come right away. After, it'll be too late." He said: "Ya know yer handsome?"

My teacher said that I was getting off topic. My teacher said that I was digressing and I was neglecting my hero.

I said: "But…"

She did exactly what the one from last year did: "Tut-tut."

I said: "It was the rain…before…after…" I said: "The trail, like in the movie, is the big river…" I said: "The monster is him. The Ornithorhynchus… the one floating on the river…"

She said: "…a shirt with sleeves?"

I said: "Yes. And boots…and that hides in the same places as kids."

She said:

"Tut-tut" and, ignoring all her "new pedagogy" techniques in order to make fun, she took the class as her witness. She said:

"Children…I think that the Ornithorhynchus in this absurd story gets clothes from department stores and, since our young friend seems to have abandoned his plan, Mister Marlon Brando has surely gone back to Hollywood." The students laughed.

In my composition, I didn't write:

The war is lost. I didn't speak. I stood there, just next to the room attached to the house and the wind blew as the autumn wind blows. They had just finished supper. Yes, I think that in the addition, the Shadows were eating their dessert like they do when they don't go out. It was Sunday and they don't go out on Sunday. I didn't dare enter. My hands were covered in mud and I didn't know how to say: "May I go wash up?" All of a sudden, I had forgotten that the verb "to be able to" had that form.

At supper, I wasn't hungry. And as I was to help myself, I just took a little plate and that was enough. I thought: "If I want more, I can always take more." I thought: "The others are going to say"...but I wasn't hungry enough to take another helping and the Shadows just ignored me. They're at the age where they only look after themselves. And I said it like it was.

At supper, I sat down at the table and when he arrived, I stopped talking. It was getting late. There was no salad left and I've already said that the last days of summer are short. I can also say that the darkness comes quickly at this time...earlier than at the beginning of the summer, that's for sure. I didn't find the words. I stopped talking. As for the monster, the monster's breathing and the sadness of the monster who says I'd like to drown myself, I didn't talk about them.

They wouldn't have believed me. He'd say Windsor, he'd say Detroit... and when he'd say Windsor or Detroit, it was as if it were much better over there. I've already said that the monster must have known the power of words.

He was bigger and stronger; he kept saying words in English, words in French... I didn't know how to fight back.

He kept saying that he had relatives in Windsor, always *ready*. He kept saying that there wasn't nothin' but treeless fields around these parts.

The worst thing was my problem with words. For some time now, my voice, my tongue, my lips and my mouth don't respond to my orders like before the summer. It's odd to say this. It hurts me and it surprises me. I still have my *Petit Illustré*, but at school the teacher says: "Speak louder." At home they say: "He's pouting today…"

It's funny; it's hard to say and almost always unexpected. Sometimes, it's too far away, and sometimes, it's just on the edge of my lips and it comes out all at once. And it's so surprising that the others don't have the time to understand what I had to say, and I can't do anything about it. And yet, that's the way it is. I try to analyze it, but…all things considered, it's better not to think about it too much, I think. When I think about it, it's worse than when I don't think about it. That's what I've noticed.

When it gets dark out, I have trouble sleeping, just like when our dog was hit by a car. It was an old dog that didn't have a pedigree or anything, but I saw it lifeless on the edge of the gravel between a layer of asphalt and the dirt ditch, and I had trouble sleeping that night. I must say I was much younger. Slowly, I used to bring my hand to my mouth and would bite down on my fingers.[17] My mouth would open and close for no reason and my fishbowl, once the lights were out, was cold and sad just like in the depths of the sea.

Autumn brings with it something unchanged which would make us believe that after the summer storm, life has once again become what it was before.

I've already said it, but I believe that it's important to come back to it. The worst wasn't the pain in my underwear: the worst was the problem that I had with words.

My voice, which before hummed beautifully like a spinning hula-hoop, has become rough and raspy for some time now – it's stupid to say, but there you have it – often I don't know how to speak and how to stop talking either…and this, in equal proportion. This is at least what I think. And I make mistakes with words. Instead of this one, it's that one that comes out. Most often, it's a similar word but that doesn't mean anything at all. And I don't know when to speak.

Yesterday, I said *valeur* (value) instead of *voleur* (robber), *vrai* (true) for *plaie* (wound), *jeune* (young) instead of *juste* (just)…when I wanted to say: "It's not just or right." Today, I said "a decision" when I wanted to say "a denunciation"…and all this worries me, I think. But I can't say it, no more than when we were in summer.

For the rest of my body, it's alright. I walk, I watch, I go to school and I don't cry.

My fate is tied to the colonel's in my plan.

I didn't say this, like the hero in my war film: *I was stuck. Washington and the U.S. sergeant on one side, the Abandoner and the Ornithorhynchus on the other. I am Marlon Brando.*

I didn't write, either:

I believe they killed me.

ENDNOTES

1 *Couchette* is a mispronunciation of *fourchette*, meaning "fork."
   Bacul is a dialectal word from the North of France used to speak
   of a "singletree," commonly referred to in French as *un palon-*
   nier. This term designates a wooden bar swung at the center
   from a hitch on a plow or wagon and hooked at either end to the
   traces of a horse's harness. *Caltron* is a deformation of *carton,*
   meaning "cardboard box." These terms are mentioned again in
   subsequent pages.

2 In the original French, the word used is "taisance" – an invented word – derived from the verb *taire* – to make silent or to
   be quiet (in its reflexive form). This verb is a homonym of *terre,*
   land or earth in French.

3 This is a reference to Germaine Guèvremont's 1945 classic
   novel, *Le Survenant.* It has been translated as *The Outlander.*

4 The word used in French is *tarie,* which contains the same letters as the verb *taire* (to be quiet).

5 The verb in French is *pouvoir.* It can also be a masculine sub-
   stantive *le pouvoir,* which means "power." Elsewhere in the
   novel, Charles forgets certain conjugations of the verb and is
   thus effectively "disempowered."

6 *Zezon* is a term that the author used as a young boy, which
   means "dumb." *Petuite* is a term no longer used, meaning
   "vomit." *Jouquer* is a verb used in Quebec and the West of
   France, which means "to perch on something."

7 The term used in French is *rallonge.* According the author, he
   chose this term, as he felt *cuisine d'été* was too long. A "summer
   kitchen" is a room, often attached to a house, in which food is
   prepared so as not to contribute to the heat in the main building.

8 The French verb *nettoyer* means "to clean." See Note 1 for an
   explanation of the other words.

9 The verb in question is *venir*, meaning "to come." This verb is used by certain people in Quebec to speak of an orgasm. In France, the verb *jouir* is used to this effect.

10 The term used in French is *risée*. This term can also mean "laughing stock."

11 *Mon voleur* translates as "my thief." *Nouère* is an old form of the word *noir*, meaning "black."

12 The term used in French is *faucheuse*. This term can also refer to the "grim reaper."

13 Capharnaum was a fishing village situated on the north shore of the Sea of Galilee. The village is mentioned several times in the New Testament. The term is also used in French to refer to a messy, cluttered and obscure place. The term was used by Homais, the pharmacist in Gustave Flaubert's *Madame Bovary* (1857), in order to designate his medical cabinet. In Quebec literature, the term is used by Léon Chicoine in Gérard Bessette's *Le Libraire* (1960) to refer to the secret room filled with censored books in his bookstore.

14 The term used in the French is *joual*. This word, which designates colloquial French in Quebec, is a deformation of the word *cheval*, meaning "horse." The coinage of the term is often associated with journalist André Lauren-deau.

15 The term used in French is *queue*, meaning "tail." This term is also used to designate a penis. Although Charles and Him are dealing with a mare, the masculine gender for horse in French and the usage of the neutral pronoun *ça* while referring to the animal evoke this appendage, especially given the sinister nature of this scene.

16 The term used in French is *ange cornu*, meaning "horned angel." This term is however a homonym of *ange corps nu*, meaning "naked angel body." As such, we chose "li'l devil" as it would seem to refer in an ironic fashion to the diabolical nature of the future event.

17 In French, the expression *se mordre les doigt* (to bite one's fingers) is used to express "regret" and is the equivalent of "to kick oneself."